PUSSY

ALSO BY HOWARD JACOBSON

FICTION

Coming From Behind
Peeping Tom
Redback
The Very Model of a Man
No More Mr Nice Guy
The Mighty Walzer
Who's Sorry Now
The Making of Henry
Kalooki Nights
The Act of Love
The Finkler Question
Zoo Time
J: A Novel
Shylock is My Name

NON-FICTION

Shakespeare's Magnanimity (with Wilbur Sanders)
In the Land of Oz
Roots Schmoots
Seriously Funny: An Argument for Comedy
Whatever It Is, I Don't Like It
The Dog's Last Walk
The Swag Man (Kindle Single)
When Will Jews Be Forgiven The Holocaust? (Kindle Single)

HOWARD JACOBSON

PUSSY

with illustrations by

CHRIS RIDDELL

JONATHAN CAPE
LONDON

3 5 7 9 10 8 6 4 2

Jonathan Cape, an imprint of Vintage Publishing,
20 Vauxhall Bridge Road,
London SW1V 2SA

Jonathan Cape is part of the Penguin Random House group of companies
whose addresses can be found at global.penguinrandomhouse.com.

First published in the United Kingdom by Jonathan Cape in 2017

penguin.co.uk/vintage

A CIP catalogue record for this book is available from the British Library

ISBN 9781787330207

Typset in 11.5/15.5 pt Dante MT by Jouve (UK), Milton Keynes
Printed and bound in Great Britain by Clays Ltd, St Ives PLC

To Donald Zec – the best of talkers,
the best of listeners, the best of friends

How is it possible to expect that Mankind will take Advice, when they will not so much as take Warning?

Jonathan Swift

F

PUSSY

BOOK ONE

REVELATION

And I stood upon the sand of the sea, and saw a beast rise up out of the sea . . .

And the beast which I saw was like unto a hyena; and his feet were as the feet of a clown; and his face was as the face of a spoiled child . . .

And the people gave him his power, and his seat, and great authority . . .

And they worshipped the beast, saying: Who is like unto the beast? who is able to make war with him?

And there was given unto him a mouth speaking foolish things . . .

And he opened his mouth in blasphemy against truth . . .

And it shall come to pass that all who dwell upon the earth shall wonder that they worshipped him . . .

And they shall know that the beast came not out of the sea but their own hearts . . .

And they shall fear that once let out, the beast will never be persuaded to go back in again.

PROLOGUE

The March of Ignorance

Early one morning in the famously hot winter of 20** a figure could be seen walking between the tallest obelisks and ziggurats of the walled Republic of Urbs-Ludus. He was looking for the Palace of the Golden Gates and was assured he would not miss it. He was a lean man in his middle forties, of more than average height but lacking hair. Though most of the people he passed pretended not to feel the heat and remained buttoned-up and scarfed, he carried his overcoat over his shoulder. Something about him – it could have been his shaved head, for this was a society that set great store by fantastical coiffure – suggested intransigence and maybe even a fall from authority. He was Professor Kolskeggur Probrius and had, until the year previously, been head of Phonoethics, a university research programme looking into the importance of language to ethical thinking. The words we used and the way we expressed them, he argued, affected the thoughts we had and the actions we took. 'Bad grammar leads to bad men' hardly does justice to the subtlety of his thinking, but that was the gist of it.

A bachelor of austere habits, he had earned the esteem of students on account of his dedication to their improvement. Then came the Great Purge of the Illuminati, and Professor Probrius found himself accused of cognitive condescension, that is to say of making a virtue of possessing expert knowledge. Students were distressed by the perceived distance between his attainments and their own. They were made to feel inferior to him and looked down upon. It was conceded that he made efforts to lead students out of perplexity by finding other words for those they found distressing, but that had only resulted, they submitted, in making them feel remedialised. The moment he claimed ignorance of the verb 'to remedialise' was the moment that sealed his fate. There it was: he believed language belonged to him. At a specially convened hearing of the Thumb Court seventy-seven thumbs went down while only two went up. Thumb Culture made no provision for abstention. Professor Probrius was out of a job.

It was as the instructions had promised. He could not miss the Palace of the Golden Gates. It was taller by at least a dozen storeys than all the other ziggurats, it bore the name ORIGEN in large letters above the entrance and then again at sky level, and it had golden gates.

Buses were already congregating in the concourse outside the Palace, spilling lucre-tourists who marked it in their *I-Spy Book of Monoliths* before being driven off to the next one.

A protest was taking place in what appeared to be a designated protest pen. From the spirit in which the demonstration was being policed, Professor Probrius deduced it was a regular occurrence and posed no immediate threat to the building's security. As the symbolic focus of the Republic's satisfaction in itself, the Palace had been the scene, three years previously, of the first of the Artisanal Bread Riots, the most violent public disturbance in the Republic's history. For years, the only activity in Urbs-Ludus had been the construction of towers. Nothing else was made. Even the bread was flown in from somewhere else and invariably arrived stale. Sick of white sliced loaves, dry muffins and inelastic pizza bases, the populace demonstrated in such numbers that the authorities had to import a labour force of skilled dough-makers from countries outside the Wall. But there was an unexpected consequence. Soon, Urbs-Ludus woke to the realisation that the Republic was flooded – not with artisanal bread but with artisans.

One section of the population turned against the other. The wealthy had their brioches but the poor had to queue in hospitals behind those who made them. Crime increased – petty larcenies at first, but then offences against the person, especially against women whom, it appeared, many artisans had never previously encountered, at least not in the immodest dress considered appropriate, in the Republic, for the wives and daughters of property developers. Viewed within the Palace as further proof of man's insatiable ingratitude, this latest disgruntlement was permitted to express itself, quietly, where it could be monitored. But there could be no doubt that the populace – albeit a different social stratum thereof – was on the growl again.

Professor Probrius had come to the Palace to be interviewed for the position of tutor to the Grand Duke of Origen's second son – but now, due to unforeseen circumstances, the heir presumptive – Fracassus. He introduced himself at reception, where they looked so affronted to see him not wearing a coat that he thought it wiser to put it on before taking it off. Security was strict but smiling. He was required to show three forms of identification and leave his smartphone in a pigeonhole marked 'Information Transmission Devices'. Two security officers patted him down, one for one leg, one for the other. A third, wearing a face mask, asked him to say 'Ah!' into a balloon. There was no knowing what means the latest enemies of the Game Economy, whether artisanophiles or artisanophobes, would deploy next, and germ warfare, passed from mouth to mouth, could not be ruled out. Professor Probrius exhaled. 'Ah!' The balloon filled but didn't change colour. No one seemed to have expected it would. Then he was invited to take a seat. Above the reception desk was a painting in the style of Titian showing the Grand Duke playing golf with the Pope. Professor Probrius shook his head as though it were a kaleidoscope and he wanted to change the shapes in it. There was so much light reflected from the crystal chandeliers that it was possible he was not seeing what was really there. But no: there, leaning on his silver putter, was the Grand Duke of Origen, and opposite him, and laughing, with a cardinal standing in as his caddy, was the Pope. The only remaining question was whether the painting commemorated a real event or a fantasy one.

Eventually he was shown up in a lift to the 117th floor and ushered into the presence of the Grand Duke and Duchess. Though they'd been sitting at a table playing the board game Cashflow, which the Grand Duchess, wanting a quiet life, always allowed the Grand Duke to win, they were dressed and primped as though in expectation of a film crew, the Grand Duke powdered and wearing his medals, the Grand Duchess, more powdered still, in a vertiginously low-cut sequinned evening gown that appeared to be entirely open, but for a paper clip, on one side. She must have had her perilously high high-heel shoes off because she was still sliding into them as he arrived. Professor Probrius, not wanting to stare at her feet, counted her ribs. She was taller than the Grand Duke by a head and Probrius thought, from the appreciative glances the Grand Duke from time to time threw up at her, that he liked this and wouldn't at all have minded had she been taller by two heads. Both had hair the colour of lemon custard, the Grand Duchess's long and irritably girlish like Alice in Wonderland's, the Grand Duke's layered as though to resemble the millefeuilles now on sale in good patisseries throughout the Republic. Professor Probrius couldn't tell how old they were. The expression 'eternally youthful' popped into his head. The Grand Duchess had had the usual surgery done on her breasts and looked wearied with all she had to carry.

Professor Probrius was greeted familiarly, the Grand Duke clapping him on the shoulder as Probrius imagined him clapping the Pope on the eighteenth tee.

'Bitterly cold outside today, I hear,' the Grand Duke said.

Probrius wasn't sure how to reply. He was a man of principles, but one of those principles was not to make an unnecessary enemy of the powerful.

'I haven't found it so, Your Highness,' he replied. 'But then it's possible I carry my own eco-climate around with me.'

'You are a lucky man, Professor,' the Grand Duke said. 'We have nuclear heating in the Palace, but we still freeze. I have put out an order for all our staff to wear an extra cardigan today.'

Such is the power of suggestion that Professor Probrius fretted briefly for the Grand Duchess, who would have been exposed to the cold had it not been hot.

She smiled, noting his concern and pulled her gown together.

'The Grand Duchess, too,' the Grand Duke said, 'must carry her own eco-climate around with her. She won't hear of throwing on a cardigan.'

Professor Probrius wasn't sure if a compliment to the Grand Duchess's hardiness was called for. Fortunately, she came to his assistance before he could frame one. 'It would be nice, Professor,' she said, inching forward, 'if we had a photograph. We photograph all our guests.'

Professor Probrius assumed this was a euphemism for another security check and readied himself for saying 'Ah!' again, but the royal couple simply positioned themselves on either side of him. The Grand Duchess fished about in her reticule, found what she was looking for and shot out an arm. Were arms answering the law of dynamic evolutionary process and getting longer, Probrius just had time to wonder before the Grand Duchess said 'Smile.' Then, laughing, she took a selfie.

Above them, on a bank of monitors, the Grand Duchess could be seen taking a selfie of herself taking a selfie in triplicate.

Walking with a slight skipping movement reminiscent of a girl on a hopscotch rug, she led the way into an adjoining room where a grand tea table was set as though for a delegation of a thousand. A ten-tier porcelain tea stand replicating an Origen tower spilled children's party food – cupcakes in pastel colours, mini hot dogs, bagel snakes and potato men with Smarties for eyes. Probrius was offered a milkshake and invited to pick his own colour straw.

Through the heat haze, the room offered magnificent views of the city. 'It's from this window,' the Grand Duchess said, 'that we look down on our competitors.'

'My wife, Professor,' the Grand Duke said, 'has a colourful turn of expression. It comes from being born in another country and reading books. Competitors is not how I think of them.'

There followed a complicated description, with which even Professor Probrius found it difficult to keep pace, of the meritocratic system that awarded titles to developers in proportion to the height and luxury-quotient of the hotel complexes, apartment blocks, shopping malls and the like which they had erected. Thus, while a couple of condominiums and an out-of-town gaming resort might get you a baronetcy, it wouldn't make you a viscount. Things had come a long way, he reminded the Professor, from the Monopoly they had all played as children, where a modest bungalow on your property could bankrupt your opponent. The Grand Duke himself was in the fantasy market today, and kept his title on the understanding that he'd go on dazzling the discontented with bright lights, inner-city ski-runs and infinity pools. It mattered not a jot that they could never afford to stay in one of his fortified hotels. It was enough that they knew of their existence. To his son Fracassus would fall the burden of extending the scale of irresponsible development – irresponsible in the sense of unconfined – set by the House of Origen.

'He means increasing the profits,' the Grand Duchess put in.

She pronounced the word with such a proliferation of fffs that Professor Probrius wondered if it had another meaning in her native country. He also wondered whether, at some level in their marriage, the Grand Duke and Duchess were at war.

'My wife,' the Grand Duke continued, 'is a mother. She worries about the pressure on her son. The higher Fracassus climbs, in her eyes, the further he has to fall. But men only fall because they lose their concentration, spread their interests, notice other things; Fracassus has no interests and notices nothing. When we play Monopoly he throws the dice as though they're hand grenades. He builds a city while I'm languishing in jail. Forgive me if I take pride in him. He isn't as other boys are. He doesn't waste time collecting stamps, listening to music or telling jokes. It's to his credit that he doesn't get a joke. Fun for Fracassus is victory. Play for Fracassus is war.'

The Grand Duchess stole a glance at Professor Probrius, as though to forge an early alliance of the sensitive.

'So,' the Grand Duke pronounced, once tea was cleared away. 'Shall we get down to business?'

'Certainly,' said Professor Probrius, finding his most charming smile and thinking how wonderful it was no longer to be in a university environment and having to watch every word he uttered. *'À nos moutons.'*

The Grand Duke looked to the Grand Duchess and the Grand Duchess looked to the Grand Duke. It was as though, whatever the nature of their struggle, they were as one again and had unanimously decided, that very minute, that they had found the right man.

'Let's be on first-name terms,' the Grand Duchess said.

Probrius inclined his head. 'I'm Kolskeggur, Your Highnesses,' he said.

'And we are the Grand Duke and Duchess of Origen,' the Grand Duke replied. 'Now here's our little problem . . .'

CHAPTER I

In which Fracassus, heir presumptive to the Duchy of Origen, is born

As the birth of potentates in the walled Republic of Urbs-Ludus went, the birth of Prince Fracassus was not especially auspicious. No thunderbolt struck the Palace. A star never before seen did not appear brighter than a meteor in the morning sky. Lionesses did not whelp in the streets. If anything, it was a quiet day. The Grand Duke arrived home earlier than usual from golf. It was not the Grand Duchess's first lying-in, so – although they say the pain of childbirth is soon forgotten – she knew what to expect. She screamed only once, causing the Grand Duke to set down the comic pages of his newspaper and carefully run his fingers around his hair. Anxiety flattened it. 'Make sure she has all the books she needs,' he phoned through to the midwife.

Then he rang his stockbroker-in-chief. 'It's about to happen,' he said. 'Buy. Unless you think we should sell.'

He waited for a telegram from the Prime Mover of All the Republics but none came. He shouldn't have been surprised. Executive power in the Federation of All the Republics was vested in commoners who looked down their noses at the petty titled meritocrats who ran their individual Republics like medieval fiefdoms. At the same time they chafed against the popularity which these Grand Dukes and Duchesses enjoyed by virtue of their showy wealth. The people gloried in their titles. Gasped at their cloud-capped towers. Gaped at their gold. What did the Prime Mover and his bureaucrats have to rival this? They passed unpopular laws and skulked in low-rise offices on an apron of mulchy marshland which the Monopoly aristocrats called the Pig-Pen and wouldn't have bought had their dice landed on it every time they threw. The Pig-Pen, as a matter of interest, was also the name the Executive gave to the concentrations of towers and ziggurats where the Grand Dukes and Duchesses conducted their business lives. Each party, when it inveighed against the ineffectiveness and corruption of the other, spoke of Mucking Out the Pig-Pen.

There was, in short, no love lost between the Federation's competing oligarchies, and so no telegram congratulating the Grand Duke on the birth of a second son on whom the future continuation of his dynasty depended, was sent.

The Grand Duke was asleep when Prince Fracassus was born.

There was a reason for this lukewarmness. Fracassus had an older brother. Jago. Of Jago everything had been expected but none of it delivered. Once bitten, the Grand Duke contained himself. He was not a bitter man. The Republic of Urbs-Ludus, as overseen by the House of Origen, promoted petty grievances not grand resentments and as Grand Duke he had to be forever setting an example. He would not rail against enemies or fate. And he would not again tempt either by showing the size of his expectations.

Thus neither longed for nor dreaded, but no sooner incarnated than hosanna'd – for he was, for all to see, an Origen, with the tiny eyes indicative of petty grievance, the pout of pettishness, and a head of hair already the colour of the Palace gates – Fracassus came griping into the world in expectation of every blessing that a fond father, a copper-bottomed construction empire, a fiscal system sympathetic to the principle of play, and an age grown weary of making informed judgements could lavish, short, that is, of a sweet nature, a generous disposition, an ability to accept criticism, a sense of the ridiculous, quick apprehension, and a way with words.

Of these deficiencies Fracassus lived the early part of his life in blissful ignorance. How different was he, really, from the usual run of children? No baby is magnanimous; all infants have thin skin; small boys will often mistake boisterousness for mirth and bullying for wit; and wordlessness, as is well known, is something children grow out of at different rates. Many a great orator begins life as a tongue-tied toddler, indeed the greatest orators in Urbs-Ludus's history remained that way.

So Fracassus's parents had no reason to notice anything amiss and they too lived in blissful ignorance of his shortcomings, if shortcomings they could be called. He was an ordinarily pugnacious, self-involved and boastful child, not much attentive to the world around him and used to getting his own way.

Visitors to the Palace did what visitors to palaces do and doted on the heir presumptive. That he took not the slightest notice of any of them was evidence both of his self-sufficiency and the richness of his interior life. That he cried the moment he was denied whatever it was his little fingers reached for only proved his resolution. That he never spoke a word they recognised suggested he was already master of innumerable foreign languages. That he spat and spewed and farted in their company only showed his indifference to the world's opinion.

It hardly needs saying that in a republic whose power resided in the spell of awe and majesty it wove around its citizens, the Internet enjoyed high esteem. The Great Duke lent his name to a dozen blogs and funded any website that promoted values close to his heart – the freedom to drink sugary drinks, to choose an example at random. Of these, the foremost at the time of the Grand Duchess's lying-in was Brightstar, a platform for nativist, homophobic, conspirationist, anti-mongrelist ethno-nationalism which might have caused greater concern to people in high places had they only known what any of those words meant.

Brightstar saw the advantage in associating itself with Prince Fracassus from the moment of his birth. Indeed, it charted his development with such sycophancy that some subscribers to the site weren't entirely sure whether they were a reading a paean to the Prince or a parody of him. Was there a difference, anyway? However to understand it, the Prince's extraordinary untutored mastery of foreign tongues was painstakingly explored. Noises he had made were phonetically laid out and readers were invited either to guess at their meanings or confirm, should they be speakers of those hypothesised languages themselves, their lingual accuracy. At this early age, Fracassus was already becoming an inspiration, an example to the people of what freedom from instruction could achieve.

In one of those brief political reversals to which any truly original site is subject, Brightstar was compelled to cease publishing for a while and some of its pages were lost beyond recovery. So there is no way to confirm that on the Prince's second birthday his water was bottled and, for a nominal sum, offered to subscribers, together with a certificate of authentication in his own hand. Porcelain pillboxes containing samples of his ordure the same. Some say this is malicious fabrication but there are people who claim to have purchased one or other or both and to have them still.

Among the Grand Duke's and Duchess's closest friends the usual jealousies stood in the way of adulation on quite that scale. A little more animation wouldn't have gone amiss, they muttered among themselves. A prince wasn't expected to show intellectual promise, but wasn't this Prince slow beyond the usual meaning of the word? And those eyes – were they ever going to open? But out loud they voiced only praise. 'He will be an ornament to your Dynasty. He will be a flower in the garden of the Republic. He will be a prince among princes.' The Grand Duke liked the idea of his son as 'ornament', wasn't sure about 'flower', but took strong objection to that equalising 'among'. His son, he hoped, would leave the others in his wake. The rest were not princes but ten-a-penny princelings, as ineffective as that *ancien régime* from whom, along with weak chins and syphilis, they'd borrowed their titles. Some couldn't even afford to live in their own tower blocks.

Concealed in his contempt for minor Monopoly aristocrats was a gnawing consciousness of inferiority that could only be explained as shame at being a Monopoly aristocrat himself. The Grand Duke looked down on everybody except those who looked down on him – the gubernatorial classes, unpropertied, untitled, unnoticed by the media and often badly dressed, but wise in the ways of governance and exercising an influence which couldn't be quantified but for that very reason attracted a near mystical envy and respect. For all his wealth and eminence, the Grand Duke had never met the Prime Mover of All the Republics, whose pronouncements, though delivered from an undistinguished address, were listened to the world over.

The Grand Duke was stung.

Secretly, his ambitions for his son were unbounded. The name of Origen could climb higher yet into the empyrean. Fracassus would build betting halls of such magnificence that only gods could afford to play in them. But after that . . . after that the Grand Duke looked to his son to Muck Out the Pig-Pen, seize the levers of power, and win for the House of Origen the mystical respect which had so far eluded it.

And then they'd see who'd spurn the advances of whom.

The Grand Duke did not lack realism. His was a republic within a republic, admired and emulated, yet for all its devotion to innocent indulgence, it had always had its critics – mumblers and fly-posters, half-day insurrectionists who sat down on rubber yoga mats and read their messages. There was no violence; it was hard to be angry outside the Palace of the Golden Gates. The building made people smile. They enjoyed looking up and feeling dizzy. Even the homeless liked to see where other people lived. But recently, encouraged by the success of the Artisanal Bread Riots, these demonstrations had got more boisterous. The Grand Duke was a lover of social platforms, but these too spread disaffection, stoking envy and encouraging the unhappy to pick publicly at one another's scabs. Follow-my-leader discontent, he called it.

In one chill corner of the Grand Duke's mind crouched calamity. The ladder was tall and the snake was slippery. You couldn't count on staying at the top. But by the same logic, nor could the Prime Mover. Thus was the Grand Duke able to see, in the very thing he feared, the very thing he craved: the Pigs cleared out of the Pig-Pen and Fracassus atop the world.

Behind their hands, people close to the Palace said the Grand Duke's natural optimism blinded him to the truth about his son's character and abilities. Others thought he had shrewdly read the age and knew precisely what it demanded: the last person for the job could easily turn out to be the first person for the job.

The Grand Duchess was too wound around in sorrow to have a view about the infant Fracassus either way. She found him hard to like, and kept away from him as a kindness to them both.

Meanwhile, Fracassus frolicked pettishly on the arboreal roof terrace of the Palace of the Golden Gates without an apparent care in the world. The sun shone, the orchards grew big with fruit trees, other towers sprouted all around without ever taking light from his, the servants brought whatever he desired, and only bouts of boredom – which he was unable to describe in words – cast a shadow on his happiness. Since he had no company his magnanimity was never tested, nor did he learn what it was to be mocked or teased. To relieve his feelings he sometimes pulled down the Lego edifices he'd built and threw the bricks off the roof. (Like Samson himself, Brightstar commented. A reference that was subsequently pulled when an editor pointed out who Samson was.) At other times Fracassus tore up the flowers in the flower beds, but no gardener dared remonstrate with him about that. All living things were his and he could rip at them as he liked. When he looked in the mirror he saw what his mother – when she was in the country – told him he was, namely a beautiful boy with a cherub's complexion and spun gold hair from which he would be able to make whatever shape his ingenuity fancied.

CHAPTER 2

Concerning a father's fears and a tutor's skirt

But then the time came, as it must in the life of every child, gifted or not, to be removed from the condition of baby celebrity – where every burp and bubble is taken as an earnest sign of future greatness – to the obscure literalism of the schoolroom, where marks are awarded for performance and promise counts for nothing. Punching, biting, scratching and swearing, Fracassus descended from the roof terrace with its infinity pool, its sandpit, its swings and roundabouts, its giant television, its bar serving baby cocktails, hamburgers and candyfloss, and the constant attendance of reporters and photographers from Brightstar, to the classrooms of the lower Palace, to questions, comprehension tests, and words. For Fracassus this was a tailspin into darkest hell. Words! Until now he had whimpered, exclaimed, ejaculated, and whatever he had wanted had come to him on a golden platter amid praise and plaudits. So why, he wondered – or would have wondered had he possessed the words to wonder with – the necessity for change? The enormity of the shock, for any child, of having to go from pointing to naming cannot be exaggerated. But for Fracassus, for whom to wish was to be given, it was as catastrophic as birth. To have to find a word to supply a need is to admit the difference between the world and you. Fracassus knew of no such difference. The world had been his, to eat, to tear, to kick. He hadn't had to name it. The world was him. Fracassus.

He had had no friends. He was the Prince. Princes proper have no friends. Jago had been too preoccupied in his search for self to be a brother to him. And in a sense he didn't have parents either. The Grand Duchess, when she wasn't travelling on business with the Grand Duke, was locked in her reading room, turning pages and letting her mind drift. Reading was an auditory experience for her. The leaves of her favourite novels fluttered between her fingers and as they did she could hear the wind blow through the enchanted forest. Sometimes she would turn only to turn back again, letting the pages sigh to her of danger then of rescue, rescue then of danger, back and forth. The books she loved best were printed on the finest paper, as diaphanous as fairy wings. They might float from her they were so slight. But when she snapped a volume shut she could hear the castle gates crash closed. Hush! She was alone. Wild beasts prowled. Who would come to her assistance now? Help, help!

For all his ambitions for his son, the Grand Duke was barely any better acquainted with him. He was too absorbed in his idea of Fracassus to notice him in actuality.

It's also possible he was frightened of him. The boy's uncanny, he sometimes thought. He lacks charm, he lacks looks, he lacks humour, he lacks quickness, he lacks companionableness, and yet he's arrogant! He didn't doubt that these absences would one day be the presences that got Fracassus noticed, but until then the Grand Duke had to find a way to live with him as a father. This he did by travelling overseas as often as he could.

There was talk on every floor of the Palace about the meaning of this parental dereliction. Some of the servants tried to be sorry for the boy but their pity foundered on some quality in him that repelled affection in any form. The word 'obnoxious' was starting to be whispered in the lifts. Nox was a far-off colony of the Republic that was seldom visited. Its inhabitants were reported to be querulous and slow-witted and to have small hands. People disliked for those or a host of other reasons were thought of as obnoxious – coming from Nox. Could that have been the real reason the Grand Duke and Duchess kept their distance – that they too thought of him as a visitant from Nox?

Hitherto, with no one listening or keeping an eye open, with no one prepared to doubt that his brain brewed extraordinary mental projects and that he spoke of them in arcane tongues to people unequipped to understand, the absence in him of the wherewithal to construct a sentence or progress a thought had gone unnoticed.

Until now.

The tutors into whose hands he'd suddenly fallen, like a god toppling from high estate into a fiery lake of devils, grasped the enormity of their task at once. Fracassus was not only short of words, he seemed to be in a sort of war with them. Had he only been surly they would have employed methods designed to relax him, make him feel safe, and communication would soon have followed. But he already was, in his surly way, communicative. He would answer their questions. He would sometimes even essay something in the nature of rough play, though he would immediately shrink should anyone play rough games back. The problem was that he seemed to feel he could get by well enough with the words he had and any attempt to teach him more was an attack upon him personally. Furthermore, he failed to see, since his tutors had words and they could do nothing better with their lives than teach him, just exactly what words had to recommend them. Did he want to end up like them? He believed himself to be complete. Ineducable because there was nothing more he would need to know – and certainly nothing more these failures could ever teach him – for the life he intended to live.

'You're all prostitutes,' he told them once.

And on another occasion, he called them 'whores'.

They didn't know whether to commend him for his loquacity – prostitute was the longest word they'd heard him use, and whore the most surprising – or discommend him for his misogyny.

As time went on and Fracassus's education didn't, his tutors acknowledged they were in a ticklish situation. They were paid handsomely to bring the boy up to scratch; alerting the Grand Duke and Duchess to the fact that scratch was still a long way beyond him would have been self-destructive. Whose fault, in that case, was that? Who but they could be to blame? The argument they prepared in their own defence, without accepting that there was anything to defend, went as follows:

> Fracassus is an independent child with an original mind. His thoughts, we are pleased to report, are unhampered by that dependence on received opinion which we often see to be the price paid by those who are overly articulate, language-crammed or well read. Since words come to us infected by assumptions of which even the most self-conscious can remain unaware, the more disengaged from language a man is, the more connected to his own heart we can rely on him to be.

The chief architect of this argument had been Dr Cobalt, the only woman on the team of Fracassus's tutors. A graduate of three universities and holding degrees in two soft subjects and one middlingly hard, Dr Cobalt was tall and slender like a snowy egret and made flustered men think longingly of the cool and even icy climates of the past. She had been the Grand Duke's choice. Being masculinist by inclination – a hunter before he was strong enough to shoulder a rifle, a boxer before a glove tiny enough for his little fist could be found – Fracassus, his father believed, would surely benefit from contact with her gentler virtues. They all would. The Grand Duke, as evidenced by his taste in domestic architecture, was epithetical by nature. And everything about Yoni Cobalt suggested adjectives. She had long hair, big eyes, full breasts, and wore high heels. And every adjective cried out for an adverb. She had very long hair, very big eyes, very full breasts, and wore very high heels. That she could have been a very successful catwalk model or children's television presenter made her decision to sacrifice herself to the bringing up of Fracassus the more estimable. Her senior on the tutorial staff, Dr Strowheim, commended her in moderation to the Grand Duke and Duchess, but repeated as though it were his own argument that their son was enriched by what he didn't know.

Whether Dr Cobalt was right to have mentioned to him and other members of the teaching staff that the Prince seemed more interested in looking up her skirt than in learning the difference between an active and a passive verb, was another matter. 'It would depend,' Dr Strowheim had jested, but with a distinct note of caution, 'on how actively he looked.'

'Pretty actively,' Dr Cobalt said.

'But it was only a look?'

'As opposed to what?'

'As opposed to a more physical exploration.'

'It was only a look, though the last time he looked I did fear that it presaged—'

'Then let's say it was passive,' the Doctor put in finally.

It did occur to him to suggest she wear trousers in the future, but trousers on women were implicitly banned in the Palace – the Grand Duchess was known not to own a pair – and, if he were to be honest about it, he would have missed the skirt himself.

CHAPTER 3

In which language is discerned to go backwards

Dr Cobalt slept badly as a rule, but on the night following her ingenious submission to the Grand Duke and Duchess that their son was brilliant by virtue of all that made him stupid, she didn't sleep at all. The night was hot – that had something to do with it. There were mosquitoes in January, a month in which, once upon a time, it would have snowed. And her basement apartment in Origen Lower Mansions, which abutted the Great North Wall of the Republic, was stuffy and noisy. The air conditioning, which the management refused to service because there was no need of air conditioning in winter, spluttered and wheezed. There was a low level of continuous noise, too, from small protest groups camped outside the Mansions, voicing their entitlements, though it wasn't always clear what they felt entitled to. Somewhere to live, seemed to be the sum of it. Whatever they could lay their hands on, Brightstar said. Promote rights instead of duties and this was the result. But it wasn't the mosquitoes or the sound of people exercising their entitlement to feel entitled that kept her awake. It was guilt. She believed she'd failed in her pedagogic duties, failed the boy, failed his parents, and failed her sex. The words prostitute and whore had continued to make appearances in his conversation, though never in a context that rendered either of them appropriate. Otherwise wordless, he seemed to want to say these words simply for the sake of saying them, as though he heard an unholy music in them. Shouldn't she, for his sake and, even more, for women's, tackle him on this?

'You can put your computer away, Your Highness,' she told him one morning soon after her sleepless night, 'and your play pad and your phones. Today we are going to have a game of synonyms.'

'How do you play that?'

'I'm going to give you a word and you're going to give me another word that means the same. So if I say lesson . . .'

'I say boring.'

'Well, that's more what you think of a lesson than another word *for* lesson. But let's continue. So, if I say teacher . . .'

'I say failure.'

If he were a man I'd throw burning tea into his face, Dr Cobalt thought. But she had to go on. Bait the line. Flick the rod. Reel him in. 'OK, so now let's try woman.'

'Ah no, not woman,' he boomed. He knew the loudness of his voice irritated Dr Cobalt. Some mornings she had to get up in the middle of a lesson to take a pill. He gave her migraines. Though he liked looking up Dr Cobalt's skirt he didn't much like the rest of her. Behind her back he mimicked the way she put her hands over her ears and closed her eyes when his volume was too much for her. Once he'd seen a film on television in which a black servant, wanting to escape a telling-off, had run out of the kitchen with her apron over her head. He combined Dr Cobalt and the black servant in a routine that would have made him split his sides had he been capable of even callous merriment. 'Oh, lordy, lordy,' Dr Cobalt cried, lifting her skirts and covering her face with them. 'Oh, lordy, lordy.'

Fracassus wished he had a friend to share this with. A girl, preferably taller than him, with custard-yellow hair waterfalling down her back and false breasts, who would run around the room with him, mimicking Dr Cobalt, with her skirts over her head.

'I'm waiting,' Dr Cobalt continued. 'Woman . . .'

He tilted his head and pushed his jaw out, something else he knew she found distasteful. It was surprising, even to himself, how much he knew about Dr Cobalt's likes and dislikes. He'd watched men on television panel shows expertly pressing women's buttons. It wasn't hard. You just had to know which faces to pull while they were speaking. 'Girl,' he said.

'Anything else?'

'Lordy, lordy.'

'Lordy, lordy?'

'Lordy, lordy, Miss Scarlett.'

'You've lost me there. Explain.'

'Can't.'

'Why is it amusing you?'

'You remind me, that's all.'

'I remind you of whom?'

He shrugged and dropped a pencil under the table.

Dr Cobalt knew what that was about. He was always dropping pencils under the table. 'You can leave it there this time,' she said. 'Keep going. Another word for woman . . .'

She waited. And waited. Was he playing her? Had he rumbled her game? Come on, she thought. Come to Momma. And at last he did.

'Prostitute.'

'Interesting. I believe I've heard you use that word before. But it doesn't mean woman does it? A woman can be a prostitute but not every woman is a prostitute.'

'Every prostitute is a woman, though.'

'Well even that's not true. You can have a male prostitute.'

'Like a faggot?'

'Not necessarily.'

'Like what then?'

'We'll come back to male prostitutes. Let's stay with the women for now. What other words for prostitute do you know?'

He thought a long time. Wherever he is, he is enjoying being there, Dr Cobalt thought. Finally he came up with whore, then tart, then hooker.

She looked down the holes that were his eyes. 'You have more words for prostitute than you have for woman,' she told him. 'I want you to ask yourself something. Why can't you think of a woman without thinking of a prostitute?'

'That's unfair,' he boomed and pouted all at once. He poked his finger at her. Frightening, she thought. One day that finger, coming out of the murk of befuddled hurt, would inspire fear. It did already.

'Why are you poking your finger at me?'

'Because it's so unfair. You asked me. This is your crooked game.'

Crooked? That was a surprise. Didn't you have to understand the concept of straight before you could understand the concept of crooked?

But he was right. She had exceeded her brief. It wasn't her job to root around in the unruly attic of the little monster's head. She was a teacher not a priest. She wasn't paid to catechise him into obscenities. She should end the lesson now.

But some imp of perversity wanted its way with her. She would fill his head with prostitutes until it burst. 'Courtesan. Strumpet. Harlot. Concubine. *Fille de joie*. Hetaira . . . Shall I spell that for you?'

She stopped, realising how this would look to someone watching the lesson on CCTV cameras. *I'm teaching your son some new words for prostitute, Your Highness . . .*

How had this happened? Dr Cobalt had three degrees from the Republic's finest universities. How had the wordless abortion got her into this?

She slept badly again. Or maybe she slept too well. She had a vision that may have been a dream. Or was it that she dreamed she had a vision? In it Fracassus had been elected to the highest position in the Republics. He stood on a great stage with his face on television screens hundreds of feet high behind him. Crowds cheered his name, breaking it up into syllables – *Frac-Ass-Us . . . Frac-Ass-Us . . .*

'I know a lot of words,' he was telling them, waving the vocabulary book she had advised him to keep and jutting out his jaw.

'Tell us!' the people shouted.

'Tart. Strumpet.'

'More!'

'Concubine. Courtesan. Nobody has more words than me.'

Dr Cobalt killed a mosquito crawling across her face.

CHAPTER 4

Concerning the part played by television in the education of a leader

No sooner had the moon orbited the earth for the 200th time, counting from the hour of his birth, than Fracassus woke to find himself fifteen.

He now began to pass the time he wasn't looking up Yoni Cobalt's skirt staring into screens. Thanks to the extensive measures the Grand Duke had taken in recent years to interface and platformise the Palace, there was not a corner of it that was not connected to walls of light-reflecting surfaces that multiplexed between security monitor, cinema, television, computer, games console, smartphone, and every other peripheral device his IT advisers recommended, thus enabling Fracassus to go from room to room in a flicker-induced trance. In this he was not much different from others of his generation for whom the screen had replaced the dummy as pacifier and the cot mobile as soporific, but with this difference – what Fracassus saw when he looked into a screen was not just any flickering image but a flickering image of himself.

Whether it was because of the size of the monitors his father had installed – some of them so big they extended beyond the confines of one room, down the passage and into another – or because he was still in the receptive as opposed to the proactive stage of his development, the Prince preferred watching himself on television to accessing any of the connectivity media at his disposal. Television spoke to him. Television told him not what the world could be but what he could be in it. Television shaped his ambitions. Self-appointed guardians of culture, such as Professor Probrius, were inclined to speak well or ill of television as though it were a single, indivisible thing; but one could no more say that television was good for people or bad for people than one could say a book was. It depended on the book. Fracassus had never read a book but he had, by the age of fifteen, watched so much television that, had it been food, he would have been confined to his bed weighing 500 kilograms.

But to say he watched unceasingly is not to say he watched uncritically. A strenuous if unconscious system of discrimination determined the patterns of his viewing. Whatever was combative and divisive he liked; whatever was discursive and considered he didn't. Whatever demeaned, amused him; whatever ennobled, roused his ire.

A list of the programmes that excited him and the programmes that left him cold can be supplied upon request; suffice it to say that he rated pictures above speaking, pictures that moved quickly across the screen above pictures that moved slowly, and action above stories. Where a drama did engage his interest it was because its hero was a bully. Bullying being the dramatic element he looked for first, he wasn't always able to distinguish a play from a panel show, or a reality programme in which contestants were fed food that made them vomit from a documentary set in the death row of a penitentiary. Whatever featured boastful winners and cringing losers, he watched with avidity. Wrestlers, racing-car drivers, boxers, condescending chat-show hosts, drug dealers, mass murderers, Tony Soprano, Max Schmeling, Macho Man Randy Savage, Henry VIII, sadistic surgeons, bent cops, the Discovery Channel's dictator of the week – it was on the shoulders of these that he grafted his own image.

In this, again, he was assuredly no different from the many millions of viewers for whom television was a stimulus to envy and emulation, except that they went about their business the following day forgetful of what had transfixed them the night before, whereas Fracassus woke possessed of the same ambitions with which he had gone to bed. There were times when he was unable to tear himself away from his imaginary reflection for long enough to go to bed at all.

His parents were shocked, on their return from a long official trip outside the Walls, to find their son much changed. He had grown somnolent, podgy, ill-mannered and, even by his own standards, uncommunicative. Though he knew of their imminent arrival and might have been expected to be at Golden Gate One to greet them, he barely registered their existence when they entered the great living room and discovered him stretched out like an odalisque on a Chinese dragon sofa, eating nachos and cheeseburgers and watching a drama about the life and loves of the Emperor Nero. When they coughed to announce their presence he waved them away with a backward movement of the hand – a reverse royal wave of the sort usually employed for the dismissal of importunate servants. 'Shush,' he said. 'Not finished.'

'How long has this been going on?' his mother demanded of Dr Strowheim.

'The series began to air about five weeks ago, Your Highness,' was his reply. 'I believe it has another ten months to run.'

'I am not talking about the series. We do not leave our son to your care in the expectation that he will be left to watch pornography.'

'It is history, ma'am.'

'History? If that's history I would rather he knew nothing about it.'

'We have done our best,' Strowheim assured her, 'to protect the Prince from knowledge it isn't in his interest to acquire, and we have acted on your instructions with regards to books. Let him read about wizards and dragons like other children was your command, and my staff have been scrupulous in not deviating from it. But he seems not to be interested in wizards *or* dragons. Since there is little literature of any other sort available to a person his age, we thought not to close down the only alternative avenue for his native enquiringness to take. He must know something about the world, Your Highness.'

'I will talk to the Grand Duke about this,' was the Grand Duchess's imperious reply. 'But I shouldn't have to remind you that you were hired to keep the world and its controversies out of my son's education until he is ready for it, not thrust it upon him while he isn't.'

Dr Strowheim would have liked to say that *The Life and Loves of the Emperor Nero* was hardly 'the world and its controversies', but he knew when to stay silent. He bowed and the Grand Duchess went off to discuss these developments with her husband.

In truth, she blamed him for the comatose state in which they found their son. Men and their gadgets! She had stood out against her husband's digitalisation of the Palace, firstly on aesthetic grounds – she hated all those wires – and secondly because she believed it was a woman's job to make the case for interpersonal relationships – too much time looking at screens, she believed, affected men's ability to read emotions, and God knows they were bad enough at it already. But the Grand Duke had defeated her, as he always did. 'One,' he told her with triumphant patronage, there would be no wires; 'These days, my dear Demanska, machines speak to one another wirelessly. It is quite marvellous, really, how technology has advanced. Which country was it that used to say it ruled the waves? I, my dear, no matter where I walk in the Palace, have only to punch a four-digit password into any device I happen to be walking past, to rule the airwaves of the world. And all without a wire to be seen. That's one. Two: reading emotions has gone far enough, in my opinion.'

He looked at her steadily and caressed her cheek. Forgive his cruelty in referring to this, but did they really want Fracassus to go in the direction of his older brother Jago, a child they no longer saw and seldom talked about but who had gone off the rails as a consequence of what the Grand Duke could only call empathy overload, reading emotions left, right and centre until he no longer knew which emotions were his own – his gender neither – and now lived they had no idea where or with whom as Joyce? No. Whatever his wife thought, he was not prepared to let that happen to Fracassus, even if it meant the boy getting fat, knowing nothing of interpersonality, and thinking he was Nero. Better Nero than Norma.

The mention of Jago always quietened Demanska Origen. Had he been her fault? Certainly he had been more her child than her husband's, and more her child than Fracassus would ever be. Was it because she blamed herself for Jago's defection that she had been less of a mother to his younger brother? Could it be that she had grown afraid of her power to sensitise? She tried to remember when she'd last looked Fracassus in the face. Yes, she'd praised his beauty. A mother had to do that. She had carried him in her womb. She had cried at his delivery. But had she ever truly looked deep into his eyes? Did she even know what colour his eyes were? But Jago, lovely Jago, she had known too well. How his face had lit up when she read to him of chocolate factories and magic schoolboys. His tutors had worried that he was still reading about the chocolate factories and magic schoolboys he'd loved at the age of nine or ten when he was nineteen or twenty, but Demanska Origen hadn't minded that. She was still reading about them herself.

She brought her worries up at her reading group. Should she have encouraged Jago to read something else?

There was a long, troubled silence. They were all mothers of sons. Daughters would find their own way into literature, but the route was too thorny for boys, especially in the face of discouragement from their fathers. Jago wasn't the only son to have lost his way. In recent years the craze for interpersonality – imported somehow from beyond the Wall, despite the strict protectionism in place – had wreaked havoc among young men. Fathers were afraid to pin medals on their sons' chests, not knowing what they'd find. The reading group wasn't clandestine exactly, but it was unclassified. The men knew of its existence and laughed among themselves. Women! Women and their feelings! But individually they feared it. What expressed itself as a feeling today expressed itself as a deviancy tomorrow.

The Grand Duke wasn't the only one pressing for the Walls to be built even higher.

The mothers, too, knowing how suspiciously their meetings were viewed, were apprehensive. Women of supreme authority and confidence in other spheres of public life, they shook when they held a book and read to one another from it in quiet, childish voices. Demanska Origen's question hardly did anything to settle their nerves. *Something else*! They shifted in their seats, rearranged their skirts, and exchanged anxious glances. Chocolate factories and magic schoolboys constituted a monotheistic faith. To wonder if there was *something else* to read about was like asking a Christian to take up worshipping the Devil.

At last the Duchess of Oblaxa found the courage to ask, 'Such as?'

The next silence lasted until the end of the session.

Demanska Origen went home to some degree consoled. She had nothing to blame herself for. She could not have done other than she'd done. Sometimes you can overexcite a child's imagination with literature. It's a risk you have to take. If she'd done anything wrong it was only that.

CHAPTER 5

A painful chapter containing matters it were better to remain silent about

Renzo Origen was more concerned about Fracassus than he had let on to his wife. But for different reasons. If the boy had grown indolent and self-satisfied while he'd been away it was no great matter; a few rounds of golf now he was back would put that right. The off-handedness, similarly, didn't much matter. He saw it as a sort of teething, his son practising the incivility he'd need in later life. But there was such a thing as overdoing it. The Grand Duke was not himself a discourteous man. He tipped his caddy well and pretended to listen when his chauffeur told him of his troubles. But he knew that those at the bottom of an empire expected disrespect from those at the top and even loved them for it. It proved the efficacy of a system of which they were part. And since few people intended to remain where birth had placed them, it gave them something to look forward to. In the meantime, they connived in their own humiliation as though the longing to be returned to the condition of a slave was a given of their natures. What was a tyrant, when all was said and done, but the embodied will of the people? If Fracassus's ambitions tended to the tyrannical, his father had no objection. But there were subtleties to be discerned in the early careers of even the most monstrous of despots. The people craved disrespect but you had to creep into their hearts first. Fracassus lacked finesse. He made enemies too quickly.

And then there was what his wife had reported to be the boy's inclination towards the pornographic.

'It is classical pornography, he's been watching, Your Highness,' Dr Strowheim had been at pains to point out.

'Pornography's pornography,' the Grand Duke replied. 'It has no place in the making of the sort of leader I intend Fracassus to be.'

This wasn't primness speaking. It was what the Grand Duke called Fun-Politik. Pornography threatened innocent soft-core sexploitation. It handed the enemies of harmless good times a weapon.

To the boy himself, sitting him down in his office on the 180th floor and turning off every television in the building, he set out his position.

'I assume you know why I've brought you here,' he said.

Fracassus pouted.

'Is that a yes?'

'Yes.'

'Yes what?'

'Yes I do.'

'Yes, *Father.*'

'Yes, Father.'

'So why have I brought you here?'

'To whip my ass.'

'I could have done that in your room.'

'Then why did you bring me here?'

'It's because I don't want your mother to overhear this conversation. You respect your mother, don't you?'

'When I see her.'

'Are you missing her? Is that why you're watching men doing filthy things to women?'

'I'm not.'

'So what are you watching?'

'Nero.'

'Why?'

'I like him. He makes people do what he wants.'

'And do you think it's right to make people do what you want?'

'Right?'

'Allowable? Kind? Fair?'

'If you're the boss.'

'Do you ever feel sorry for these people?'

'Why should I? They get what's coming to them. It's fun, seeing people scared.'

'By people do you mean women?'

'Some.'

'And does this Nero make them do sexual things?'

'Dad!'

'Well?'

'Some of them.'

'And that turns you on?'

Fracassus buried his face on his father's desk.

'Listen,' Renzo Origen went on. 'It isn't easy being a man. Especially a rich man. Women come on to you. They come on to me all the time. But you have to show them respect. You'll be able to have all the women you like, but you don't have to hurt them. Think of them as collectables rather than conquests. I'm not saying you shouldn't let them know who's boss occasionally. Woman like to be mastered. They say they don't but take my word for it – they do. Nobody will mind that you're red-blooded. Men will envy you and even militant women won't hate you in their hearts. I've slapped many a feminist's bottom, I can tell you. And been thanked for it. But don't get into weird shit – you know what I mean?'

Fracassus raised his pinhole eyes and shook his head. It suddenly occurred to Renzo Origen, looking into his son's plump vacancy, that he hadn't understood a word that had been said to him.

'Describe to me,' he said, 'what you think of when you see a woman.'

'On television?'

'In the flesh.'

'I don't see any women.'

'You see your mother.'

'Not often.'

'What about Dr Cobalt? You see her.'

Fracassus was finding it hard to swallow.

'Well?'

'Well what?'

'What do you think of when you see her?'

Nothing from Fracassus.

'In one word.'

Fracassus scratched his head with one hand and patted his hair with the other.

'You can tell me. I'm not going to be angry.'

'Pussy,' Fracassus said.

That was when the Grand Duke of Origen decided it was time to rethink the direction his son's education was taking and call in outside help.

CHAPTER 6

In which it is agreed not to scare the horses

'So that, not to conceal anything from you, Professor, is our problem,' the Grand Duke declared, opening his hands as though to show his cabinet of painful secrets was now empty. 'Our son is an original. He is the coming man. But it is hard to imagine him, as he is, soothing shareholders or buying off interest groups. Soon he will have media pouncing on his every word. He has to have words for them to pounce on. You may wonder why we are not sending him to college. I mean no disrespect to your profession, Professor, but the academy is not for everyone. It does not teach what we would wish him to learn, and what it does teach we would wish him not to. You wear your erudition lightly, Professor, but there are some it incapacitates for any job but incapacitating others. Fracassus's fulfilment will lie in giving pleasure not in causing pain.'

Professor Probrius smiled and made a pyramid of cogitation with his fingers. This had been one of the gestures that had cost him his job. 'It would seem to me, Your Highnesses,' he opined, 'that you are of two minds about your son's vocabulary. On the one hand you would like him to be capable of more sophisticated discourse, such as will flatter those who are of his party and persuade those who are not; on the other you fear, as any parent might, what infections he will pick up from language as it is commonly deployed by people aggressively unsympathetic to your way of life.'

'You put it well,' the Grand Duke replied, 'though we are not backward-looking. A benign commercial plutocracy of play cannot be run on democratic lines, but where the people's wants don't run counter to our own, we indulge them. I am not their nanny, but in the matter of the few precious rights left to them after generations of liberal interference – the right to smoke wherever they choose, the right to consume cheap fuel, the right to live in single-colour communities, the right to drink sugary drinks, the right not to have wind farms in their back gardens, the right to fritter away their life savings at my gaming tables – I am their champion. I don't scorn their tastes. They enjoy reality TV. So do I. So, I suspect, in your secret heart of hearts, do you, Professor. And if Fracassus is likewise entertained, where's the harm? It keeps him on a level footing with those whose lives will one day be his to play with. It can only be a bonus if he speaks to them in words small enough for them to understand—'

'Without,' his wife interrupted, 'meaning to imply that the people are deficient in understanding—'

'Exactly,' the Grand Duke continued. 'Without meaning to imply any such thing. But when they discover how alike they are despite apparent differences, they will love him.'

'But—' interposed his wife again

Professor Probrius showed he was all attention.

'But – but, he will not be loved by anyone, however small his words, unless he can express himself more sympathetically. He must at least learn to conceal the indifference he feels towards everybody but himself.'

'My dear—'

'No, Renzo, we must be honest. We have nurtured a brute.'

'Not a brute.'

'A brute!'

'Because he doesn't read, my dear . . .'

'He does read. He reads the comics you buy him.'

'Because he doesn't read what you think he should read . . .'

'I am his mother. I have a right to an opinion on his reading.'

The Grand Duke commended himself for not saying, in public, 'And we know where that leads.'

'What it comes to,' he said instead, 'is that the Grand Duchess and I want Fracassus to be brought up to speed, not just as a speaker but as a man, but not so up to speed – I'm sure you understand me – that he acquires concepts that are destroying our society. You should know that Fracassus has an older brother—'

'No!' cried the Grand Duchess.

'Then maybe you should not know that Fracassus has an older brother. Forget I've said anything. But let us at the very least agree on this – personal experience has taught us that you can have too many words.'

The Professor nodded. He was familiar with the argument. 'It is strange,' he said, 'that we have a derogatory term – pleonasm – for the use of more words than are strictly necessary, yet don't have a laudatory term for the use of fewer words than are strictly necessary. But the truth is, it isn't quantity that's the issue. What we need to find for the Prince are the *right* words. And these we must select with sensitivity. There's a saying in the teaching profession: don't scare the horses. Of late we have been scaring them half to death. You tell me Fracassus doesn't often, for security reasons, leave the 170th floor of the Palace; I fear the spirit of the times would reach him were he to live sealed up on the 1,000th. He, too, we must treat as we would a frightened horse.'

Professor Probrius could not have answered more felicitously had he tried. For the Grand Duke and Duchess, the Prince's employment of the wrong words was as much the problem as his having no words at all. Only recently, after the most minor altercation with his parents, Fracassus had pushed his face out, curled his lips back, and aimed at them, as though they were bullets, the words 'Fuck, nigger, cunt.'

They had called the royal physician who examined him over a period of weeks. 'He has, Your Highness,' the physician reported, 'what I'd call Tourette's, only without the Tourette's.'

'Will he get better?' the Grand Duchess asked.

'In the sense of will he extend his range of pejoratives? He might, Your Majesty.'

So Probrius's proposal that they select the right words for the Prince with sensitivity was warmly welcomed.

'And we think that you, Professor,' the Grand Duke said, looking across to his wife for confirmation, 'are just the person to sneak the right words in. I hope you won't mind if I am kept abreast of the situation. I might have a few words of my own to suggest. And occasionally one or two I would like to see withdrawn.'

'I too,' the Grand Duchess said. There was a great sadness about her, Professor Probrius noticed. He wondered if she were homesick.

Or was there simply – given that the most sorrowful of spirit are the first to notice sorrow in others – a great sadness about him?

He bowed, all three shook on the arrangement, and the Grand Duchess took another selfie.

Professor Probrius was given a free hand with the disposal of Fracassus's existing tutors. He dismissed them all with the exception of Dr Cobalt.

CHAPTER 7

A wind blows through the Republic of Urbs-Ludus

Of the many perversities to which our species is subject, wanting the worst to happen is perhaps the strangest. Only wanting to be looked down on by the powerful comes close to it. Kolskeggur Probrius, though he personally wanted to be looked down on by nobody, did hope for the worst for everybody else. The violence visited on his Phonoethics course had left him embittered and vengeful. So the signs which he read in the wind that the university that had expelled him was a spent force – not just his university but every university – gave him a wicked pleasure. In its demise he espied his vindication. Anything he could do to speed the process up, he would.

He was a man who wet his finger and held it out to the wind. He liked to know which direction it was blowing from and relished being the first to warn of the damage it would do. In the ancient world he'd have been respected as a wind-prophet, but to moderns he was just a desponder. He had tried to prepare his university for what was coming – *beware the people!* – predicting that everything educators had ever meant by education – example, elucidation, emancipation, deliverance – would soon be scattered like dead leaves. He had proclaimed this at his Trial by Thumb. He might as soon have slit his throat on the steps of the Student Union. He pronounced 'people' without respect and down went half the thumbs. He pronounced 'education' with reverence and down went the other half.

He descended from his post in a waterfall of blood.

Well, none of it mattered any longer. The Republic wasn't listening to its universities. They were beyond a joke. Even the most second-hand of the Republic's comedians had stopped looking to safe rooms and trigger warnings for comic material. The universities were abandoned cities. Single-identity tribes wandered the corridors, speaking words the rest of the Republic didn't recognise. They might as well have put bones through their noses, and some of them did.

Professor Probrius put his finger to the wind and read what it was saying. Soon, the purgers would be purged in a carnivalesque revolt against protected attitudes, correct ideas, all the things you were not supposed to say, all the things you were not supposed to feel, all the hard-won decencies and easily enunciated pieties, all the sanctimony, all that was holier than thou, and with it all that was civilised. Gone – the victim of its own provocations – gone, on a day not far removed from this one, maybe in a year, maybe in ten years, but gone without a doubt, in one great gust of wind.

The sooner, Professor Probrius thought, the better.

He wasted no time settling into his new post. Before meeting Fracassus he thought it wise to exchange ideas with Dr Cobalt.

'Yoni,' she said, giving him her cheek.

'Kolskeggur,' he responded.

'I gather from your sanguinity,' she said, 'that you haven't yet had the pleasure of seeing the Prince with your own eyes.'

'I haven't. But his distraught parents have described him to me with some vividness.'

'Nothing beats the real thing.'

'I'm sure it doesn't. You, I understand, have been here a number of years.'

'Five. He was ten when I first had the pleasure. He hasn't disappointed.'

They were in a coffee shop by the Eastern Wall and so had nothing to fear, they felt, from cameras or microphones. But even so – perhaps the precaution was a leftover from his university days – the Professor scanned the ceiling. 'I gather,' he said, 'that you don't exactly feel in loco parentis to the boy.'

Dr Cobalt screwed up her arctic eyes. 'Even his parents don't feel in loco parentis to the boy.'

'Let me play the devil's advocate. Aren't we, in that case, obliged to feel sorry for him?'

'Normally I would respect your advocacy. Empathy was one of my degree subjects. But there are times when the usual rules of pity don't apply. I too once subscribed to the philosophy that a child is a blank canvas on which parents and society write their own messages. Before that, I even believed in the sacredness of the infant, trailing clouds of glory in the moment of his delivery into a harsh and godless world. The Prince, I have to tell you, trailed a cloud of shit.'

Professor Probrius smiled and looked around him again, just to be sure. He couldn't remember ever having liked a woman so much on first acquaintance. 'I take it, then, that you don't much . . .' he began. They both knew the joke.

For her part she was surprised the Professor was not more affronted by what she had to say. She'd decided she would not hold back, though candour could easily cost her her job. She did not know what loyalties the Professor was bringing to his appointment. She had read some of the papers he had written, from which it was impossible to deduce what kind of man he was personally. Pedantic, of course. But then so was she. A teacher who wasn't pedantic wasn't a teacher. So she had hopes for him. But she was taken aback, nonetheless, by the alacrity with which he embraced her view of the task before them. He even appeared to be energised by how much they would have to do to make a human out of a monster for whom not a shred of pity could be found.

That said, he was evidently not himself prepared to be as outspoken as she was. How could he be, given that he was yet to meet the boy? But she felt that reserving judgement was and would go on being his modus operandi. Fine with her, so long as her modus operandi could go on being revulsion.

'I should warn you before you meet him,' she said, 'to be prepared for how ugly he is.'

'I think you've already conveyed that.'

Was he being stern with her after all? Her tongue, she knew, could run away with her. Especially when she was out of the Palace of the Golden Gates.

'I don't mean morally ugly. I mean facially ugly. One can escape a person's ugliness by looking into their eyes. There at least there might be beauty. But Fracassus has no eyes to speak of. It could be because he sees imperfectly that he juts his jaw out. His natural movement is a forward projection of a sort I've only ever seen on a bewildered primate. And if his jaw's too big for his head, his head's too big for the rest of him, which is ironic considering how little is in it.'

'I have to say this is not the impression I get from his parents. His mother talks of him as a beautiful boy.'

'Parental love is blind.'

'I thought you said his parents are unable to love him.'

Yoni Cobalt crossed her legs and slowly brought one wing of her long split skirt over her knees. The swish made Probrius feel just a little light-headed.

'They don't love him,' she said, 'in the sense that you and I use the word love. But the immoderately wealthy, like the monarchs of earlier times they emulate, are biologically programmed to look upon whatever issues from their loins, as with whatever issues from their wallets – offspring are just another investment, are they not? – as perfect. Imperfect doesn't compute with the success they have made of their lives. Not to love what they give birth to is not to love themselves. That's why you and I are here. They fear there's been a fracture in the pipes. They can smell the shit. It's our job to fix the plumbing.'

Professor Probrius laughed. Yes, without doubt, he had never liked a woman so much, not only on first acquaintance, on any acquaintance.

CHAPTER 8

The end of stupidity

'Consider this, Your Highness,' Professor Probrius told Fracassus on their first morning together, 'as a getting-to-know-you session. But first, if Your Highness has no objection, I'll open a window.'

'You can't.'

'You mean you won't let me?'

'You can't. There are no windows. It's to stop people jumping out.'

'So how do you get fresh air?'

'I don't want fresh air.'

'What if somebody who isn't you wants fresh air?'

'They can go somewhere else.'

'Do any of your father's buildings have fresh air?'

'Ask him.'

'What about when you build? Will your towers have windows that open?'

Fracassus couldn't hide his impatience. 'Fuck, nigger, cunt,' he said.

'I beg your pardon?'

'Is this an interview?'

'I'm curious, Your Highness, that's all. I've read that you are looking forward to working with your father on a new casino with golf courses and saunas and giant televisions in the pools, and I wonder if they'll have windows that open?'

'So that people can throw themselves out when they've lost their money?'

'Would that bother you?'

'Not if they've paid the bill.'

Professor Probrius paused to write something down in his notebook. 'Talk to me about yourself,' he said, putting his pen down.

'Like what?'

'Well, you tell me. Who are you?'

'I'm me.'

'You are, but remember I don't know you yet. What are your interests? What do you like to do in your spare time?'

'Not prostitutes again . . .'

Professor Probrius looked alarmed. 'Explain that to me.'

'Dr Cobalt likes me to talk about prostitutes.'

'*Likes*? Are you sure? When did she last talk to you about prostitutes?'

'She didn't talk to me about prostitutes. She wanted me to talk to her about prostitutes.'

'And what did you tell her?'

'That I know nothing about prostitutes.'

'And what did she tell you?'

'I can't remember. Other words. Dr Cobalt is crooked.'

'That's a serious charge.'

'Don't worry, I won't tell my father. He'd lock her up if I did.'

'Would you like her to be locked up?'

'I don't care. It doesn't matter what she does. She's a failure like all teachers.'

'You think I'm a failure?'

'I don't know you yet. Probably.'

'Well, let's get back to knowing you.'

Fracassus was sitting in an executive chair at an executive desk in front of an executive-sized television monitor. He had, to Probrius's eye, the look of a small monarch of a country that had no population. 'Perhaps we should have that off,' Probrius suggested.

'I always have it on.'

'Well, for today, let's try without.'

Fracassus tapped his keyboard. On all 270 floors of the Palace, monitors coughed and went to sleep. If he couldn't watch he didn't see why anyone else should.

'OK, well that might be a good place to start,' Probrius said. 'Why do you always have your television on?'

'I like watching it.'

'Do you have any favourite programmes?'

'Wrestling. Wars. And people being told to do stupid things.'

'Who by? Comedians?'

'Sometimes. And hypnotists. There was someone on like you a few nights ago. An uptight guy. So this hypnotist gets him to take his clothes off and crawl around the floor and bark like a dog.'

'And you enjoyed that?'

'Who wouldn't?'

'What else do you enjoy?'

'The guy who makes my bed. He's spastic. He's all right when he's making the bed but when you speak to him he's like . . .' Fracassus did his imitation of a badly strung marionette to show Probrius what Megrim was like. He let his tongue loll out and dribbled.

'Aren't you sorry for him?'

'Why should I be? He's lucky to have a job. That's it.'

'Tell me about the last thing you saw on television.'

'It was a thing about Nero.'

'Not the coffee shop, presumably.'

'I don't know any coffee shops. I'm not allowed out.'

Probrius tried a little ingratiation. 'Maybe we can fix that,' he said.

Fracassus seemed not to care. 'Out' interested him, but 'out' with a professor did not.

'So the Roman Emperor Nero?'

'Him. Yeah.'

'And you liked that why?'

'The naked Roman hookers.'

'You're only saying that to shock me. Was that how you got round to the subject with Dr Cobalt?'

'You seem interested in Dr Cobalt.'

'She's my colleague.'

'Lord, lordy,' Fracassus said.

'I don't know what that means.'

Having done his spastic marionette, Fracassus could see no reason not to do his horripilated black mammy. 'Lordy, lordy, Miss Scarlett.'

'I don't recognise who you're being.'

'You should watch more television.'

Professor Probrius was content to leave it at that. They'd made satisfactory progress, he thought.

Sipping cold lemonade, Professor Probrius reported a censored version of the morning's conversation to Dr Cobalt. 'Well, whatever else he is or isn't, he's not a pushover,' he said, wiping the perspiration out of his eyes.

'I've been thinking the same,' Dr Cobalt said. She too was finding the winter weather oppressive. 'Do you think there could be some sewer-rat cunning there?'

They were eating an organic salad in a restaurant that had a lot to say for itself – a restaurant with a pleonastic menu, it amused him to think – at the far side of the city. Probrius had not wanted to go there because it was frequented by university people and he did not want to see anyone he knew and answer questions about what he was doing now. But it was a favourite of Yoni Cobalt's and, all things considered, he didn't mind being seen with her.

'I'm not inclined to think so,' he replied. 'In my experience we feel we have to grant some atom of intelligence, even if it's only vermin intelligence, to the very stupid. It's a way of castigating ourselves for thinking of them as stupid in the first place. Once it was a mark of civilisation to revel in the inanities of fools and blockheads. Now we worry about what made them blockheads in the first place – an unfair education system, some abuse suffered in childhood, a bang on the head. With blame culture comes the end of stupidity as a concept. I find it regrettable, myself, that no fool is allowed to attain his full-blown folly entirely on his own.'

Dr Cobalt put aside her salad. Probrius had gently alluded to the prostitution test she'd set Fracassus some months before – he wasn't prying, just curious – and the memory of it was still painful to her. Violation Studies had been another of her subjects at university. Probrius could laugh, but violation wasn't funny. There'd been violation the day she'd listed all the words she knew for prostitute. Of that she had no doubt. The question was: who had violated whom?

'Whatever the word for it,' she said, 'the thing he did, the thing he made me do, was damnably clever. And it's you who's just said he's no pushover.'

He stretched out a hand and laid it on hers. 'No pushover, no. But nor is a wild dog when it's cornered. As for the thing you said he made you do, I think you're attributing to him what's essentially yours. It was you who made you do it. Feeling you've been had is your act. The more sophisticated we are, the more we feel we must grant sophistication to a fool. The besetting sin of our times . . .'

Hearing himself, he paused. Is this another fine mess my punditry's getting me into? he asked himself. He wished he had an easier manner. He wished he had fewer degrees. He wished he were more of a wild dog himself. He threw the Doctor an apologetic look. He was sorry for spoiling their little tête-à-tête repast.

But he had forgotten that Dr Cobalt had a number of degrees of her own. And he didn't yet know that she had a soft spot for pedants. 'Go on,' she said, 'what's the besetting sin of our times? I'd better know in case I'm inadvertently committing it.'

'I doubt it, my dear.' And he was away again. 'What it comes to, in my estimation, is that we liberals find it so hard to bear the space we see in the minds and hearts of the ignorant that we fill it with our own compunctions. We are only this far' – he showed her the edge of his knife – 'from maintaining that the stupid are more intelligent than the clever.'

'Christianity got there a long time ago,' Dr Cobalt reminded him. 'You aren't going to tell me Fracassus is a holy fool.'

'He's a holy little shit. But . . .'

CHAPTER 9

In which Fracassus is taught an important lesson about tax avoidance and has a bright idea

The Grand Duke invested a day a week in the commercial education of his son. 'Quality Time' was the expression some fathers used to describe the intimate hours they devoted to their children; the Grand Duke called his days off with Fracassus 'Quantity Time' – a quiet opportunity for them to sit down together and discuss how much they were worth.

As a rule, these days would begin with the Morning Story, a short extract from the Grand Duke's own favourite business literature, some mornings Adam Smith, others Dale Carnegie, and occasionally a page or two the Grand Duke had written himself. He had talked for years about gathering his thoughts on acquisition and development into a small and beautifully bound volume, but nothing had come of it. Among his hopes for the future was that one day he and the Prince would write it together. In the meantime, he read passages aloud – sometimes the same passages – with which the Prince seemed most in tune. A chapter entitled 'How To Get Away With Getting Your Own Way' was a particular favourite.

It touched the Grand Duke to see his son sitting at his desk and cradling his cheek in his hand while he read to him about the ins and outs of avoiding rent control or removing a troublesome tenant. It would have reminded him of the early days of parenthood when, tucked up in bed, the infant Prince would close his little bullet-hole eyes and ask to hear a story – *would* have reminded him of such days had they only happened. I haven't been the best of fathers, the Grand Duke admitted to himself, vowing to do better while knowing he wouldn't.

No excuses, but he wasn't in the best of health. Overseeing the building of the Origen ziggurat, golf, and the tragic circumstances surrounding Jago had taken their toll. The Grand Duchess, too, was fragile and, when she wasn't locked away with her susurrating fairy stories, she needed his attention and devotion. The future held its breath for Fracassus.

This was not a parochial ambition. If the Grand Duke wasn't in the best of health, neither was the Republic. Neither was the world. When he said the future held its breath for Fracassus he didn't just mean the future of the House of Origen. He meant the future of the planet.

But he wasn't going to rush things. He understood his son's education architecturally, starting from the bottom, a floor at a time. First to the top wasn't always the winner. Hold the ladder steady; mind the snakes. For the moment at least, the Prime Mover could sleep easy.

Some days, after the Morning Story, the Grand Duke would take the Prince to inspect their properties. On his early visits Fracassus had liked going up and down in the lifts, counting how many floors he owned. Now his pleasures were of a more sophisticated kind. He liked calculating how many people he owned.

On this day, the Grand Duke had planned a visit to the Nowhere Palace of New Transoxiana. It was situated on an artificial beach whose sands were of surpassing softness, sands the colour of his wife's hair, on an offshore artificial island outside the Walls of the Republic and reachable from it only by a secret underground tunnel. Other titled personages were allowed to use this tunnel but only the Grand Duke had a key. Fracassus had never visited this isolated section of the Wall before and was surprised to see his father putting his ear to it, as though listening to its heartbeat. They had travelled to the Southern Wall without attendants, just the two of them, father and son, and if not exactly in disguise, not exactly in full regalia either. Fracassus watched as his father continued his doctorly exploration of the Wall's chest, tapping it and listening. Eventually, a tiny aperture appeared and into this the Grand Duke inserted a bronze key. A door opened, just wide enough for one person to enter at a time. It was dark when the door shut behind them. The Grand Duke carried a torch but shone it only when they lost their footing. He wanted the experience to be both a learning adventure and a rebirth for his son. Fracassus didn't do metaphor and was bored. He reached for his phone. 'You won't get a signal down here,' his father told him. 'Who were you going to ring, anyway?' 'I wasn't going to ring anyone. I was going to check the weather.' 'We're in a tunnel. There is no weather.' No weather? Fracassus was frightened. He'd seen a television programme in which a father took his son to the top of a mountain to slit his throat but then God stepped in to stop him. Not a great storyline but he liked it when the father slit a ram's throat instead. If his father was planning something similar, where was the ram? It frightened him to be without a signal.

'You still haven't told me where you're taking me,' he said.

'Offshore.'

'I didn't know we had a shore.'

'We don't. We have the idea of a shore and I'm taking you to the idea of off it.'

Ideas frightened Fracassus. 'Does it have a name?'

The Grand Duke lowered his voice. 'Avoiding tax. Not to be confused with evading tax. Evasion we'll discuss next week.'

'No, I meant does where we're going have a name.'

'The Republic Outside the Walls of the Republic.'

'So is this abroad?' Fracassus had never been abroad.

'It's not abroad when you're there, but it is when you're here. It's what accountants call abroad. Wait till you see it . . .'

'Abroad?'

'No, the Nowhere Palace. A building that is ours when we say it is, and not ours when we say it isn't. A building whose magnificence adds lustre to the Republic's reputation but not its treasury. Not everything, my son, can be judged by the financial contribution we make. Sometimes we do what we do for the pure beauty of doing it, even if that means keeping a little something back for ourselves.'

Fracassus remained silent. He had been in the dark for long enough. But then daylight began to pour into the tunnel and the excitement of arrival seized him. He would have liked it to be abroad, but offshore would do. So this was what his father meant by beauty. He thought he could smell the sea. Offshore! – why, even the sky was bluer. The Grand Duke nudged him. Look! There were only a few seconds for his eyes to adjust before Fracassus saw it, a great gaudy flower of steel and glass, growing out of the sand, a purple pyramid bearing the name ORIGEN in the usual gold lettering, and then THE NOWHERE PALACE.

Fracassus held his breath. Coloured lights danced before his eyes. At the entrance to the pyramid was a winking crystal Sphinx.

'Classy or what?' the Grand Duke said, gripping his son's arm.

'Classy,' Fracassus agreed. He had never used the word before and liked the shape of it in his mouth. *Classy* – it seemed to open a whole new world of sensation to him. It made his mouth moist. It made his cheeks hot. *Classy*. It was as though he'd swallowed the softest of chocolates.

They entered a great amethyst atrium. It was like a giant cage for jungle birds. Parrots, macaws, toucans. Fracassus had watched a nature programme about killer birds. For a moment he thought there must have been real birds there, then he realised their calls were being piped through loudspeakers, which was even better. 'What do you think?' his father asked.

'Classy,' the Prince said.

'The world's top retailers fight to get a space here,' his father said. 'Tiffany, Cartier, Chanel.'

'Is there a Caffè Nero?' Fracassus asked.

'No Caffè Nero. We wouldn't have Caffè Nero here. We have Nespresso. Now let's look at the gaming room.'

This was the biggest play area Fracassus had ever seen, even bigger than the roof garden on which he'd rolled as an infant, asking for the world and receiving it. He was sorry he'd used up all his words. If the entrance to the casino was classy, what was this?

Extra classy.

So many play tables under a single roof inlaid with gold leaf, but, more marvellously, so many players, some dressed as though for the opera, others as though they'd just come from behind a counter selling washing powders, women beautiful and plain, men sophisticated and awkward, some of either sex accustomed to throwing money around, others flat broke and apprehensive – a great, classless party of gamesters who would in no other place or circumstance find themselves together, divided by the urgency of their needs, united in the single fantasy of winning enough to make need yesterday's bad dream. Fracassus looked around him. The wheels turned, the balls jumped, croupiers employed rakes to push cards about like hot coals, one-armed bandits lit up and whirred, numbers and colours were called, men punched the air, women cried out, one threw what few chips were left to him in a rubbish bin on which the word Origen was stamped in gold leaf.

'Mine,' Fracassus thought. 'My offshore midnight palace. My party. My kingdom.'

Was this how humanity appeared to God when he looked down on it from heaven? That very question was posed in the Republic's infancy by Lodj Chjarrvak, the Republic's only thinker, just before he drove his car into the Wall. 'A mortal shouldn't own a casino,' he had pronounced as he strapped himself in. 'It makes him mad.' But no one told Fracassus this.

He slid into the great offshore garden of his thoughts where fortunes were won and lost, where killer birds called to one another through speakers, where he remembered his mouth softening around the sibilants of *classy*. Blood rushed to his lips.

The Grand Duke looked at him with satisfaction. If he wasn't mistaken, this was the first sensual experience of his son's life.

'Are you all right?' he asked. It wasn't a real question. He just wanted to hear Fracassus say he was happy.

'I think I have an idea, Father,' the Prince replied after a while. He appeared to have been concentrating hard.

'What idea, my son?'

'There are men here with winnings to burn, right?'

'Right.'

'And others with sorrows to drown?'

'That's also unfortunately true.'

'Don't you think we could do more for them?'

'You aren't, I hope, talking about psychological counselling.'

'No. Pole dancing.'

The Grand Duke took the boy in his arms. This was the moment he'd been imagining from the day his son was born. Their first business conversation. 'I think that's a brilliant concept,' he said. Then quickly threw in a qualification. 'But no touching. We don't want to fall foul of the feminists on the Licensing Board. And don't imagine you're going to run it.'

'Why not?'

'We have grander plans for you.'

'Such as?'

'You will discover in time.'

'When in time?'

'When your education is complete. And when you've travelled. I went to Egypt, China and beyond the Urals for my inspiration. The Nowhere Palace wasn't born in a day, and didn't grow out of my mind only. You too must travel.'

'Can I go to ancient Rome?'

'We shall see, my son. We shall see.'

The Grand Duke walked back through the tunnel in a state of high agitation. The trip had gone better than he'd dared hope and he didn't want to spoil the moment. He didn't speak the whole time they were underground and wouldn't let Fracassus speak either. But on coming out again into the Republic he risked giving shape to his thoughts. He looked up to the heavens and breathed the air. It wasn't clean, but what was? Done, he said to himself. That was the mercantile side of his son's education taken care of. The ambition tree had been planted. Henceforth, cupidity would water it.

Now all he had to do was fix the politics.

CHAPTER 10

How a weatherman brought sunshine into the Prince's heart

Sometimes, when a great man wants something enough, the gods or whatever name we know them by, assemble and agree to bestow it upon him. Such was the divine favour enjoyed by the Grand Duke that no sooner had he said the word 'politics' to himself than they came upon a commotion in the streets which only the practice of democratic politics could explain.

Another plebiscite, presumably. The Grand Duke held himself aloof from people politics. Plebiscites had wreaked havoc upon the Republic once upon a time but they had become so common that he knew to take no more notice of them. The people exercised their power and whatever it was they'd voted for was forgotten in the euphoria of their exercising it. The next day things returned to normal.

But voting still drew large crowds. It was like a carnival. Cars hooted in support of their side and other cars hooted back. Some drivers succeeded in tooting their horns so expressively it was as though a whole ironic conversation of automobiles was in progress. Professor Probrius, out shopping with Dr Cobalt, heard it and thought of the Persian poem *The Conference of the Birds*. The birds, finding themselves without a king, go in search of a bird who might be suitable. Might cars one day do the same, he wondered. They were driving themselves already. It wasn't fanciful to suppose they would soon be casting votes. And with no less acumen, he thought sourly, than their drivers. Dr Cobalt was on his arm. She knew of several other medieval works in which animals sorted out the tricky issue of government. Professor Probrius delighted in her knowledge. 'A particular favourite of mine, also Persian as it happens,' she went on, 'is *How the Lions Deposed their King and Instituted Constitutional Democracy*.' Professor Probrius said he hoped she knew of a good translation, or was proficient enough in Farsi, for them to enjoy reading it together. She didn't have the courage to tell him she'd made it up.

Fracassus, meanwhile, was revelling in a freedom he rarely enjoyed. For five minutes in the Nowhere Palace he thought he'd found his Nirvana, but now the tumult of election stimulated his fickle mind. He had no idea what the people were voting for. It was the uproar that aroused him, the flags, the cheering, the atmosphere of combat. He had never seen a crowd before, except from the hundred and seventieth floor of the Palace. Close up, it was another event entirely. He couldn't have known that people massed could generate such heat, or affect the way the very light was refracted. Was the ground shaking or was that his blood moving quicker through his veins? It was as though one of his favourite television programmes had come alive on the streets. Nero could have ridden through on a chariot. Fracassus heard the citizens hailing him. *Hail Nero! Hail Fracassus!*

Some among the throng put radios to their ears, though Fracassus didn't know whether that was to drown out the noise of the plebiscite or get more news of it. Vans with loudhailers toured the streets. Two buses faced off in the square, each flashing graphs and figures on giant screens, the same sum appearing now as profit, now as loss, now as what the electorate stood to gain from war, now as what armed conflict with one or other of the sister Republics beyond the Wall would cost them.

Fracassus wanted to know which bus to support. Which side would the Emperor Nero have been on?

The Grand Duke had misgivings. By politics – the politics of which it was time Fracassus gathered some awareness – he didn't mean supporting one side or another. An overview was what he wanted for his son, an ability to use words like liberty and freedom and know in a rough sort of way what they meant; how, again in a rough sort of way, they should sound; and why, in a more precise sort of way, they were never to be granted. But he didn't want Fracassus dirtying his hands by actual association. War or Peace? Without being especially enamoured of Peace, no one took the prospect of War seriously. It was just another occasion for a referendum. They might as well have been deciding between meat or fish for lunch. But that was still no reason for Fracassus to be down there mixing with the proponents of either. He was glad, at least, that they had come out without their regalia. Despite the heat he turned up his coat collar and advised Fracassus to do the same. This was not a place for a Grand Duke and his son to be seen.

'You don't have to support any bus,' he said.

'But which is true?'

There it was, the very thing the Grand Duke feared. Truth! Soon his son would be wearing the flat cap of revolution, loading the bus with explosives and driving it at the Palace.

'That depends on your angle of vision,' he said.

'Well, I like the red bus better than the blue bus,' Fracassus said. 'It's got more people around it.'

A scrawny old gentleman standing by them in the crowd overheard him. Until now he'd been waving his stick at the red bus and cackling.

He had wild hair and carried a plastic shopping bag stuffed with papers. Fracassus wondered if he was a soothsayer. In every episode of *The Life and Loves of the Emperor Nero* a soothsayer appeared wearing rags and waving a stick. There must have been thousands of them in ancient Rome. 'You like red better than blue,' he said, turning his wild eyes on the Prince. 'That's the most intelligent political statement I've heard all day. Do you hear that, Philander?' – he was shouting now at the Advocate for War, unless he was the Advocate for Peace, addressing the crowd through a loudhailer from the open top of the red bus – 'I've got someone here who understands your message. Better red than dead. Ha!'

The old man threw back his head and cackled again. Fracassus thought his neck might snap. In *The Life and Loves of the Emperor Nero* the Emperor made a practice of snapping soothsayers' necks with one hand. He did it with a little twisting gesture, like screwing the top off a bottle. There were schools in the Republic where kids entertained one another in the playground copying that gesture. *Bonum nox noctis*, you old fart. Snap! Pity poor Fracassus who, having no such friends to play with, had to make his own entertainment.

'Let me tell you something,' the old man said, turning again to Fracassus as though surprised to see him still there, 'a father should never live to see his son grow up. Look at him up there, the fraud, grinning like a choirboy and spewing excrement. He was all excrement when he was a baby and he's all excrement again. I wish it would blow back down his loudhailer and choke him. Can you hear what he's saying? The Republic is in danger. Ask him who from and he'll give you a different answer every day. Today it's the Republic of Gnossia. They're going to steal our jobs and rape our women, he says. Have you ever been to the Republic of Gnossia? They have full employment and their women are ten times more beautiful than ours. They would rather impale themselves on the Wall than even visit us. Do you know how I know that? *He* told me. What do you say to that?'

Fracassus was not accustomed to conversing with strangers. He felt himself colour. He ransacked his intelligence for an answer. He was about to say 'Fuck, nigger, cunt,' when he remembered the word he'd learnt that very day. 'Classy,' he replied in panic, jutting his jaw.

The soothsayer went wild with excitement, rolling his head so that his hair flew in all directions, gesticulating with his stick, laughing crazily.

'Do you hear that, Philander – he thinks you're classy. Another one! And all because I paid for you to have a private education.'

Hearing his name called, the Advocate raised his hand. For a split second he resembled a schoolboy waving to his father from the steps of his school. Fracassus had never been to school or even seen one but he had, without pleasure, watched repeats of *Brideshead Revisited* on television. All faggots.

The old soothsayer must have read his mind. 'My fault, all my fault,' he rambled on. 'I should never have sent him there in the first place. An academy for scoundrels who speak a smattering of Latin, that's all it is.' Then, taking Fracassus by the arm, 'Come on, come with me and we'll meet him. He can't resist an opportunity to demonstrate his charm on someone new. Hey, Philander, give your voice a rest and meet your new fan. He's a nobody and he looks too young to vote so there's no advantage to you in talking to him. That should appeal to your sense of the topsy-turvy. Don't do what's worth doing, do what isn't. Your old school motto – *Quid debemus facere oppositum*. Come down from your lying battle bus and tell this boy what you're going to do when you win the vote even though you won't.'

To the Prince's acute embarrassment, the Advocate – son or no son, excremental liar or truth-teller – descended and was among them. In a matter of seconds he had pushed through the adoring crowd and was pumping Fracassus's hand as if it were some magic trick and he the magician.

Fracassus was immediately star-struck. He knew who was pumping his hand. He'd seen him countless times on television, reading the weather forecast. So soothsaying ran in the family. The famous need only one name and Philander was his. No other weather forecaster in the Republic was better known or more loved. Not for the quality of his prognostications but for his looks, the prepubescent face, the mischievous smile, the collop of hair the same lemon-custard colour as the Grand Duke's, the Grand Duchess's, and Fracassus's own. But above all for the gleam of what critics of him called his mendaciousness. Every grin a lie, they said. But how could one complain when every lie came companioned with a grin.

Fracassus didn't watch television to pass judgement. It was true that Philander's forecasts were rubbish. Sun all day tomorrow, he'd promise, and Fracassus knew for a certainty it would rain. The channel kept him on because the viewing figures went through the roof with every deception. Fracassus was not alone in feeling singled out by him, joined, just the two of them – one behind the screen, one in front of it – in the seductive knowledge of falsehood. Of course it would be dry when he'd promised showers. Fracassus loved looking out of his window and seeing the Republic bake in Philander's empty promises.

The Prince didn't understand how he could enjoy being lied to, but he did. And evidently voters, in all likelihood not knowing what they were voting for, felt the same. Lie to us, lie to us. The first falsehood was like a declaration of love. The second a proof of it. After that – but after that didn't matter. After that Philander had skedaddled.

Fracassus let his hand melt in the weatherman's. Philander here, in front of him. Philander, whose pink, powdered fingers would caress the weather map with a strange, indecent incompetence, as though he were one baby undressing another. The Great Philander, undressing him.

'It's true what my old dad's telling you,' Philander said. 'I don't know *what* he's told you, but I guarantee you it's true. Every bit of it. Everything's true.' His eyes met Fracassus's. The boy swam in their treacherous blueness. Tomorrow temperatures could reach ninety-seven degrees, and lo! there was a blizzard. A calm night and every tree in the Republic would be uprooted. 'Say it after me, *Everything's true.*'

'Everything's true,' Fracassus repeated as though in a swoon.

'You'd better believe it,' the scrawny soothsayer shouted.

'So can I count on your vote?' the weatherman asked Fracassus.

'I don't have a vote,' the Prince said.

'Age the problem?'

'Rank.'

'Rank! So much the better. Things rank and gross in nature . . .'

'Give him your pitch anyway,' the old man said. 'Don't send him away empty-handed.'

'Everything's true,' Philander said again, 'not because it is, but because I say it is.'

Fracassus didn't have to be told to repeat it this time. *'Everything's true because you say it is.'*

During its short time in Philander's grip Fracassus's hand had felt like a fireball. Released, it was as a hailstone.

*

The Grand Duke, having lost Fracassus in the crowd, had waited anxiously for his return. 'So what was that all about?' he asked when the Prince reappeared, orange-faced and his hair somehow enfolded into itself like a napkin at a banquet.

Fracassus shrugged. They began to walk home in silence, then Fracassus said, 'Do you know what I really want?'

Cold terror gripped the Grand Duke's heart. Was Fracassus going to say he wanted to make war? Was he going to say he wanted to make peace?

'What, my son?' All his hopes waited on the Prince's answer.

'To be a weatherman.'

The Grand Duke breathed again. His son had had his first smell of politics and not been seduced by ideology into supposing it could be separated from light entertainment.

He slept well that night. His son's future was secure. This morning a pimp, this afternoon a weatherman, tomorrow the world.

CHAPTER II

A short chapter concerning bricks and mortar

Buoyed by his success in getting Fracassus to take more interest in his properties, the Grand Duke gave him a hundred acres of land and told him he could build whatever he wanted.

Fracassus drew a picture of a Roman amphitheatre.

The Grand Duke discussed the implications of this with his wife. 'It isn't necessarily,' he said, 'what it seems.'

'Nothing is,' the Grand Duchess said. 'But this just might be.'

'For all you know he might intend it as a children's park.'

'With swings and roundabouts to torture traitors on?'

'I think he has made provision for a sandpit in his plans.'

'Renzo, that will be to soak up the gladiators' blood.'

They called Fracassus into their presence and asked him how he saw the amphitheatre operating. He pushed his chin out in the manner of Nero and inverted his thumb.

'Who do you plan to kill there?' the Grand Duke asked. He was giving his son a chance. Go on, show your mother how absurd her fears are.

'Christians,' he said.

'Fracassus, this is a Christian country.'

'Jews, then. I don't know . . . Muslims . . . Humanitarians.'

'Humanitarians aren't a religion.'

'We could still throw them to the lions.'

Was he joking? The Grand Duke scrutinised his son's expression. Had there been room enough for light in his eyes, it would have been easier to tell. But no, not joking. And yet he was not in deadly earnest either. It was as though Fracassus inhabited some hitherto undiscovered zone between meaning what he said and not meaning what he said. Ambiguity, was it? No, ambiguity took cognisance of alternatives. The zone Fracassus inhabited appeared to be one where neither words nor intentions had traction. You could just say a thing, and then unsay it, with no cost to yourself and no repercussions for others, because there were no others. The Grand Duke had noted such inconsequential changeability in his dogs. They would want a walk and then they wouldn't. Changeability wasn't even the word for it. They wanted a walk in one sphere of time and being, but didn't want it in another. They were bifurcated. Being human, the Grand Duke decided, meant putting these two spheres together in a continuum of responsibility and decision. By that measure his son was not yet human.

While not wanting to put a dampener on the Prince's creativity, or provoke him into God knows what response, the Grand Duke gently suggested other uses for an amphitheatre. A running track, perhaps. An open-air auditorium for pop concerts. Fracassus shrugged. Whatever.

Eventually the amphitheatre was built and modified into an out-of-town shopping mall. Fracassus opened it. Professor Probrius and Dr Cobalt wrote a speech for him but he decided against delivering it. Instead he sliced the ribbon with an ornamental sword and inverted his thumb.

By general consent, the Amphitheatre was an aesthetic triumph.

Security staff dressed like Spartacus. Hostesses at the information booths wore thigh-length silver boots, short togas made of aluminium foil, and sported laurel leaves in their hair. A caged lion entertained the children with its roars. And Neroburgers were for sale.

Commercially, too, the Amphitheatre thrived.

'You have to admit, he has a touch,' the Grand Duke told his wife. 'For a sixteen-year-old.'

'So what does he intend next, a slave market?'

The Grand Duke looked away. Fracassus had already submitted his plans for a colonnaded plaza, the pillars to be finished in white marble, with walkways along which slaves would be paraded, space for restaurants and a Caffè Nero, and a raised stage on which the auction itself would be conducted.

Other than saying, 'In no circumstances are we going to allow you to be the auctioneer,' the Grand Duke raised no objection. The Saepta Julia was finished within budget and on time, and soon became the most visited Ayurvedic spa and herbal treatment centre in All the Republics. Slaves were available for a price, but you had to know who to ask.

CHAPTER 12

A mother worries in 140 characters

Solemnly commemorated as the dawn of seriousness in adjoining Republics, an eighteenth birthday was a joyously frivolous occasion in Urbs-Ludus. The Grand Duke marked the Prince's with a giant marzipan replica of the Palace and a mock sonorous announcement. 'It is time, my son,' he said, 'for Twitter.'

He had discussed the Prince's progress with Professor Probrius and Dr Cobalt, both of whom felt the character of the Prince was coming into clearer focus.

'He is certainly who he is,' Professor Probrius declared.

'And you can certainly see who he's going to be,' Dr Cobalt added.

'And words?'

'Yes,' said the Professor, 'there are more than there were.'

'More, without doubt,' Dr Cobalt agreed.

'And more appropriate?'

There was a pause. 'We are working on that.'

'I have myself,' the Grand Duke pronounced, 'added to his stock of commercial and political terms. I wouldn't say he was fluent in them, but nor would I say he is tongue-tied. I wonder if we might agree that he has enough to be going on with and concentrate on other skills. I think his knowledge of geography is shaky. He has told me several times that he has a yen to travel to ancient Rome but thinks it's in Los Angeles. This is a slip occasioned by confusing television epics, I imagine.'

'And while we are on that subject, Your Highness, he does also suffer chronology amnesia in relation to ancient worlds in general. He isn't entirely clear we aren't still living in them. He talks a lot about Caffè Nero. I have a suspicion he thinks the Emperor owns the chain and might actually be working in one of them. So perhaps we should look at his history, too.'

'Excellent idea. Let's get him modernised. I propose to get him tweeting.'

For someone as beguiled by screens as Fracassus, he was slow to embrace interactivity. How to explain this the Grand Duke didn't know. Perhaps the Prince had been alone with his own thoughts too long to be curious about anyone else's. He didn't miss conversation because he'd never had it, and he didn't crave the to and fro of social media because fro wasn't a preposition that called to him. What the Grand Duke had to get him to see was that Twitter didn't entail any of the tedious conversational niceties he feared. Twitter was an assertion of the tweeter's will, full stop. It imposed no obligation to listen or respond. 'You can be as deaf as a post and as blind as a bat,' he told his son, 'and still tweet with the best of them.'

Had he had the time, the Grand Duke would personally have led his son into the arts of social media self-assertion, but there were pressing commercial matters to attend to, and there was no point asking the help of the Duchess, who lacked the requisite genius for compression. She refused to understand it. 'I fail to see,' she said, when the Grand Duke explained the nuts and bolts of the system to her, 'how Fracassus is ever going to attain 140 characters. He doesn't have enough words.'

'140 characters is the maximum, my dear,' he told her.

'And what's the minimum?'

'Demanska, I have no idea. How is that relevant?'

'I would like Fracassus to keep his messages as brief as possible. I don't want him making himself ill thinking of something to say. You know how finding just one word can defeat him.'

'*Le mot juste*, my dear. One word can sometimes be enough.'

'In Fracassus's case it will have to be.'

They exchanged anxious glances. They both feared what that *mot juste* could turn out to be.

Left to his own devices, would Fracassus tweet exclusively about pussy?

CHAPTER 13

In which Fracassus informs the world what he's eating

To allay his wife's concerns – and not only incidentally his own – the Grand Duke appointed a Twitter adjutant to assist the Prince in mastering the necessary arts.

The person he chose was Caleb Hopsack, leader of the OPP, the Ordinary People's Party, and twice voted Commoner of the Year. Though not a member of the Grand Duke's inner circle – as how could he be, given his loud championing of all things unquiet and unrefined? – the two had nonetheless built up a friendship over the years based on Caleb Hopsack's knowledge of the turf and the Grand Duke's longing for some of it to rub off on him. The Grand Duke was under no financial necessity to gamble but felt ancient twinges of kinship with bookies and touts, with tipsters, with stables, with the smell of straw. Perhaps his grandfather . . . Whatever his motivation, he liked the occasional visit to the racecourse, particularly – whenever possible – in the company of Caleb Hopsack, who seemed to know everybody in the racing fraternity from owners to jockeys to punters and even to the horses. Though he had no reason to envy anybody, the Grand Duke envied Caleb Hopsack. What was his secret? How had he succeeded in making ordinary people feel he was one of them when he had amassed considerable personal wealth, belonged to the most exclusive clubs, hobnobbed with Grand Dukes, and dressed like a stockbroker's idea of a gentleman farmer who enjoyed a tipple? Certainly the Grand Duke knew no one else of his eminence who could, with such an instinctive flair for looking wrong, wear a racing trilby and windowpane check coats and yellow cotton trousers, and look right in them.

'I don't know where you find these things,' the Grand Duke once remarked, looking him up and down with undisguised admiration and perplexity. He felt uncomfortable calling them 'things' but wasn't sure what other word to use.

'The question isn't where but why,' Hopsack replied.

The Grand Duke waited. 'Why?' he asked when it became clear that Hopsack wasn't going to tell him otherwise.

'It goes without saying,' Hopsack explained, going into that third-person solipsistic mode that ordinary people found transfixing, 'that as leader of the Little People's Party, Caleb Hopsack must speak exclusively to and for the concerns of little people. To do that successfully he must look like them.'

'I thought you were leader of the Ordinary People's Party . . .'

'Ordinary/Little, Little/Ordinary – same difference.'

'But you don't look anything like Ordinary or Little people. I have met them. I employ several hundred thousand of them. None of them would know how to begin dressing like you.'

'You entirely miss the point,' Hopsack said. 'I am the idealised, never-never rural version of what they secretly would like to look like. It doesn't matter that the clothes I wear are not ones they would know how to access or could afford to buy even if they did. Sartorially, Caleb Hopsack is their shadow self. Sure it's a joke. But it's a joke they get. I bare my cigarette-stained teeth at them and remind them of a horse. They come muttering to my meetings and remind me of bags of hay. We despise one another. This is the age of the ironising of the archetype. I have a beer pot with my name on it in every public house in the Duchy but the Plebs know I prefer Scotch. They need Caleb Hopsack to be ordinary and a toff at the same time.'

'So which are you?'

'What sort of question is that? Have I not said that this is the age of the ironising of the archetype? Maybe I am the one, maybe I'm the other, maybe I'm both.'

He was just the person, the Grand Duke thought – maybe just the three people – to oversee his son's Twitter page.

With the Grand Duke's permission, Caleb Hopsack would begin by building up interest in Fracassus on his own Twitter page. It would help gain momentum, he said, if Caleb Hopsack were to be filmed chatting to the Prince outside the Golden Gates. Perhaps the Prince would be so good as to put his arm around Hopsack's shoulder, shake hands with him, kiss him on both cheeks, and then, to the camera, give the double thumb of Internet approval. Whereupon Hopsack would open wide his famous reticulated mouth and gulp down the admiration of his followers like a shark swallowing down scampi. This would go directly on to YouTube, innumerable links to which Caleb Hopsack would tweet around the world.

The Grand Duke expressed surprise that the leader of the Ordinary

Little People's Party would want to show himself – forgive the expression – jerking off on extraordinary big people.

'If you will forgive *my* expression, Your Majesty,' Hopsack said, 'you are harping on a broken string. Size is no longer relative to itself. Today, thanks in no small measure to Caleb Hopsack, things are not what they were yesterday. Everything's in the wash. Tomorrow, everything will be in the tumble dryer. Big/small, grand/common – these simple identities are over. By next year, you'll be more common than we are.'

Time was moving too quickly for the Grand Duke. 'Who's "we"?'

'The common people.'

'And what will the common people be then?'

'The aristocracy.'

'Leaving you where?'

'Still leading the party.'

Mesmerised by Caleb Hopsack's tailoring, and frightened by how wide he could open his mouth, Fracassus acceded to his every request. After his encounter with the Weatherman he had developed a taste for upside-down talk. 'I'm delighted to meet you,' he told Hopsack when the cameras began to roll. 'Unless I'm not.'

'Cut!' Hopsack cried. 'I think that's a bit too unnuanced.'

Fortunately, Professor Probrius had taken Fracassus through nuance the day before. 'From the Latin *nubes*, meaning cloud,' Fracassus said with some consciousness of erudition. There was a self-satisfaction about Caleb Hopsack that made Fracassus want to hit him. He was glad he had knowledge to do it with. On the other hand he admired him. 'I can, if you'd prefer,' he went on, 'be more cloudier.'

'Well let's not overdo it,' Hopsack said. 'This *is* Twitter.'

For the next take Hopsack asked for them to be filmed *inside* the Golden Gates. He thought it would further their common cause to give the impression that they were in his Palace and that the Prince had called on *him*. 'And . . . action!' he called, leaning against the Golden Gates and occasionally rubbing fingerprints off them with a check handkerchief. The two men began to talk about their special relationship.

Over the following weeks Caleb Hopsack tweeted praise for the Prince's dynamism, generosity, thoughtfulness, integrity, potential suitability for high office, however high that office should be. He was a good guy. Incredibly focussed. Hopsack's tweets had an air of vacant authority about them. I am confident that such and such is the case, he would say. He did not expect to be contradicted or questioned. His confidence was an imprimatur of truth. If he tweeted that the Prince was a special person then the Prince was a special person. His recommendation was enough.

Two or three months later, with Caleb Hopsack at his shoulder, Fracassus began to tweet for himself. His first attempts evinced an uncomplicated charm:

11 Nov: **Nice today.**

he wrote. And then, emboldened:

12 Nov: **Not so nice as yesterday. Cheeseburger for lunch.**
13 Nov: **My mother still nagging me about reading so my father buys me a comic. *The Prince* by Mantovani.**
14 Nov: **On page 1 of *The Prince* by Mantovani.**
15 Nov: **Cheeseburger for dinner.**
16 Nov: **On page 2 of *The Prince* by Mantovani.**
17 Nov: **My eyes hurt.**
18 Nov: **Still on page 2 of *The Prince* by Mantovani.**
19 Nov: **Demo outside Palace. Placards say WE WELCOME REFUGEES. I say shoot them.**

20 Nov: **Love it that thick morons reacted angrily to my shooting suggestion. What's wrong with these people? I was joking.**
21 Nov: **Given up reading Mantovani's *The Prince*.**

'Not bad, but now let's step the pace up a bit,' Caleb Hopsack said. 'Let's address an issue. Perhaps you could mention me.'

Fracassus did as he was bidden.

Lunch with Caleb Hopsack. He paid. Classy gesture from an incredibly classy guy.

Followed by:

Other diners incredibly interested to see us together. So gratifying.

Followed by:

Waiter said his wife committed suicide a year ago this day. Hopsack added 5% to tip. Incredibly moving.

Followed by:

Walked into demo against Miss Universe pageant. No wonder. Women marchers looked like pigs.

Followed by:

Hopsack promising ordinary people he'll get migration numbers down to minus zero if elected. Every confidence he'll deliver.

Followed by:

> **The idea that Caleb Hopsack is migrationist is almost laughable.**

'And don't forget,' Hopsack told him, 'that you can retweet.'

'Retweet what?'

'Well, my tweets to you for a start.'

Fracassus turned up for his weekly cheeseburger dinner with his parents wearing a green and ochre windowpane check tweed jacket with three vents and mustard corduroy trousers.

'Go back to your room this minute and change,' his mother told him.

'I may have started him too soon,' the Grand Duke conceded. 'The boy might be eighteen but he is still impressionable.'

'I did warn you this was bound to happen the minute he met a real person. Have I not been saying for years that all the television he watches has numbed his capacity for interpersonal relationships?'

'You can't blame television. At least he's his own self when he's being Nero. Maybe I should get him a bigger screen.'

'That just puts the problem off for another year.'

'There's no time like the future,' the Grand Duke said.

'I say deal with it now.'

'And get him to do what with his time instead? Read about wizards?'

'Help you to rip the wires out of the Palace for a start.'

'For the thousandth time – there are no wires. It's all done by electromagnetic waves.'

'Rip the electromagnetic waves out then. They're brain-cancer-forming, anyway.'

'There's no proof of that.'

'Our son's the proof of that.'

'I have a better idea. He's eighteen. You know what he needs . . .'

'Renzo, he might as well be eight.'

'You still know what he needs . . .'

The Grand Duchess turned her face away.

Later that very evening Prince Fracassus was sitting with his father in the latter's favourite gentlemen's club. No one asked questions about Fracassus's age.

If the evening saw Fracassus bobbing on uncharted waters, the morning saw him landed on a tropic isle.

He was used to waking with an erection and attributed it to the hours he'd just passed in his own company. But this morning he awoke to an unaccustomed sensation: when he looked at his erection he thought of someone else.

Great boner, he tweeted. **Must be love**.

CHAPTER 14

When my love swears that she is made of truth . . .

'After all that talk about prostitutes,' Professor Probrius laughed, 'you'd think he'd know how to find one.'

Dr Cobalt gently demurred. 'You could say that's to his credit.'

'The Grand Duke is said to be distraught.'

'Why distraught? You can't be telling me he had his heart set on his son settling down with a prostitute.'

'I don't know about "settling down". But whatever he had his heart set on, Fracassus has apparently broken it now.'

'But not his mother's, I suspect.'

'I wouldn't be so sure about that. Most mothers aren't troubled by their sons enjoying the company of women of easy virtue. They keep the channels of affection free for them. It's feminists they're frightened of.'

'Do we know she's a feminist?'

'That's the rumour. And a graduate into the bargain. Dark-haired, too. And wears trousers. A dark-haired feminist graduate with trousers and her own views. It couldn't be worse.'

The furore – for no other word could do justice to the amazement and conjecture that spread from the basement of the Palace to the 200th floor – had a simple explanation. After a conversation lasting no more than fifteen minutes, Fracassus had asked the coat-check girl at his father's club to marry him.

Prior to that, Fracassus had looked pleased enough with the company his father had found for him. Tactfully making his excuses, the Grand Duke had slid away, leaving his son in the company of women who gave a new meaning to the word classy. Tall, tanned, teetering, lustrous-lipped, generously implanted, and smelling of the best department stores, they entwined themselves around the Prince, who sat on a swing seat at the bar, swivelling to greet every new addition. They petted him. They blew in his ears, two at a time. Like butterflies skimming a flower, they brushed his lips with theirs, each passing on the nectar the others had collected. Looking for a way of describing how his mouth felt, Fracassus hit upon the image of a jam sandwich. He closed his eyes and swung his seat. Singly or in any combination his young manhood could devise, the women exhaled promise. Dr Cobalt had given him the words to describe their profession; now he had the plethorous Platonic reality of which the words were but shadows.

So why wasn't he as carried away by the women as his father had every reason to suppose he would be?

They reminded him of his mother.

That was not a reason to give up on them altogether. Fracassus was not a boat burner. On many an evening watching slave girls dropping grapes down Nero's throat he had succeeded in dispelling his mother's likeness. It was a matter of narrowing his eyes and letting the blue flicker send him half to sleep. And anyway, in Nero's world mothers and hookers freely swapped roles. So when he rose to go to the men's room it wasn't with the definite intention of not returning. But he had not counted on meeting the girl who took the coats. Rounded where the women he had left behind were willowed, dumpy where they were attenuated, to all intents and purposes blind in that she hid behind owlish spectacles where the girls at the bar had shooting stars for eyes, and wearing trousers instead of a snow-fairy dress – it must be remembered that Fracassus had never in his life seen a woman wearing trousers before – she struck him with the sort of force that persuades some men to give their lives to God. That she did not in any way remind him of his mother was, of course, part of it; but it was her voice and confidence that overwhelmed him. She had the assurance to be frumpy. She had the self-possession to be bossy. Her voice, unlike that of any woman he had ever met, including Dr Cobalt, was not modulated to please. You could take her or you could leave her. Fracassus had been waited on hand and foot, but here was someone not in the slightest bit overwhelmed by his rank or apologetic about her own. It was either punch her in the face or fall in love.

Status seemed nothing to her. He was a prince and she was a cloakroom attendant. So what? The job she was doing just happened to be the job she was doing. She wasn't defined by taking coats. What was his excuse?

Fracassus asked her to leave the coats – he'd buy everyone a new one – and join him at the bar. He was surprised by his own temerity. She frightened him, but made him comfortable at the same time. It was not permissible, she said in the most matter-of-fact way, for a person not a prostitute to join a club member at the bar. But if he wanted to wait for her she knew a little place she could take him to later. No red velvet. No crystal glasses. No tarts. 'Will other women there be wearing trousers?' he asked. She thought it likely. 'Then I'll wait for you,' he said.

Her name was Sojjourner, she told him. With a double j.

The reason she wasn't defined by taking coats, she explained over coffee in a paper cup and a cheeseburger on a plastic plate, was that she did it only to finance her studies. Fracassus looked deep into her owl-eyes and saw bookshelves. 'Have you ever finished a whole book?' he asked. She laughed inordinately, throwing back her head and rolling her whole person. 'A few,' she said. 'I'm even writing one.'

A great fear swept across the open plains of the Prince's mind. Should he ask what her book was about? What if she told him?

Did it matter? He had got to this age well enough, never understanding anyone's answer to a question. These things evened themselves out. She would never understand his world. They could not understand each other together. He saw their future: he watching a beauty pageant on television, she sitting on his knee and writing her book. Children? Yes, if he concentrated hard enough. He saw a young Fracassus watching a beauty pageant on television. And a small Sojjourner, dressed like her grandmother the Grand Duchess, winning Young Miss Urbs-Ludus.

'You've gone somewhere,' the real Sojjourner said.

'I was thinking.'

'About the women waiting for you at the bar?'

Fracassus looked away. 'They're not my type,' he said. 'They don't read books.'

'Can you be sure of that? How do you know they're not financing their studies like me? It's hard for a woman to get a grant. Prostitution is just one of the ways women get by in a man's world. From a feminist perspective, prostitution in such a case can be a valid choice and is to be differentiated from coerced sex-working, which is not to deny that it reinforces a negative stereotype of women in a way that harms both sexes.'

Fracassus wondered if he was going to faint. Not even Yoni Cobalt could put together so many letters without breathing.

'Is that what you're writing about?' he asked.

'No. The subject of my book is the constitution of the Republics with special reference to Urbs-Ludus. Its working title is *Somnolence and Corruption: A Warning to the Comatose.* Prostitution will come into it.'

Never having seen anyone like her before, and not knowing what else to do, Fracassus made to kiss her. She pulled back, raised a little finger, wagged it at him and, in the loudest voice he'd ever heard not issuing from a loudhailer, said, 'Too soon.'

Fracassus apologised and put his hand between her legs instead.

'Too soon even for that,' she laughed.

'When then?' Fracassus asked.

'I have a degree and a book to finish,' she replied. 'I have criminal lawyers to expose. I have women's health and job prospects to improve. I have children to save. I have the comatose to rouse. I have a mark to make.'

'I'll wait for you,' Fracassus said for the second time that night.

CHAPTER 15

. . . I do believe her though I know she lies

'She's called Sojjourner with two js,' he told his father.

'Sojjourner with two js? Am I supposed to be impressed? I suggest you think again with three ns.'

'Why ns?' the Grand Duchess asked.

'No, no, no and no.'

'That's four ns,' Fracassus said.

'You'd better not cheek your father,' the Grand Duchess warned. 'He's very upset about this. And so am I.'

'I love her.'

'Love her!' the Grand Duke exploded. 'What can you know about love. You're a child.'

'If I'm such a child, why did you take me to your club?'

'In the mistaken hope you'd grow up. You don't know this woman. You've spent ten minutes in her company.'

'Sometimes ten minutes are all you need.'

'You're right, and it only took us ten minutes to find out who she is.'

'I know who she is.'

'Oh you do, do you? And do you know she is a Rational Progressivist of the School of Condorcet?'

Whereupon, taking turns, the Grand Duke and Duchess led their wayward son on a grand historical tour of Rational Progressiveness, starting with the *populares* of ancient Rome – not favourites with his beloved Nero if they were not much mistaken – through Rousseau, Diderot, Kant, Hegel, pausing for support at Nietzsche's attack on Hebrew Socialism – and ending up, via Marx and Lenin, with the brutal charismatic revolutionism of Castroism, the murderous, killing-them-softly quietism of Corbynism, and the blood-soaked rice fields of Pol Pot. We bet, they said, that she never told you any of that.

'She told me she wanted women to earn the same as men,' Fracassus said.

The Grand Duke sighed. 'Ah yes, that old toxic chestnut – equal pay for women. Sounds innocent, doesn't it. But nothing ever stops at what it starts with, Fracassus. First equal pay, then paid time off for period pains, then five years' maternity leave, then nursery provision, then another five years for post-partum depression, then leave with an ascending scale of bonuses for up to twelve migraines a years, and the next thing we know the Anarcho-Syndicalists are on our backs demanding legislation to make croupiers wear flat shoes and hostesses wear trousers. And that I'm damned sure she never told you, or you wouldn't be standing here like a bitch in heat.'

'Renzo!' the Grand Duchess cried.

'What? I never mentioned his brother.'

'Renzo!!'

There being no more to be said on the subject of the Prince's brother, the couple fell silent, until the Grand Duchess felt able to start again on Fracassus. 'What we want you to understand before it's too late,' she said, 'is that you'll never be happy with her. At the first argument she'll call you a dirty capitalist.'

'Why would she call me that?'

'Because it's what you are,' the Grand Duke said. 'In her eyes.'

'She's a Metropolitan Liberal Elitist, darling,' his mother said. 'I know it hurts.'

'So what are we?'

'Scum,' the Grand Duke said. 'In her eyes.'

'Enemies of the People,' his mother added.

Fracassus rubbed his face. 'Caleb doesn't think we're enemies of the people and he's the leader of the Ordinary People's Party.'

'This is where it gets complicated,' the Grand Duke said. 'There's a war going on out there for the soul of the people. Caleb appeals to them but doesn't like them. Elitists work for them but don't appeal to them. Meanwhile we're the only ones the ordinary people really like. We're self-made – well, at least I am. We like tall buildings. We like tall wives. So do the ordinary people. It's only the Metropolitan Elite who hate us. And you have to go and find yourself one. Sojjourner with a double j, my eye. Couldn't you see that for yourself, you foolish boy? There is no double j in Sojourner. There is no Sojjourner. She invents her name and changes the spelling of it because that's what her class does.'

'She minds coats.'

The Grand Duchess found a laugh of the deepest irony. 'Ha – she minds coats. She told you that? She minds coats because minding coats makes her look like an ordinary working woman. Do you want to know the truth – you'll thank me for this one day – her family manufactures coats. Mink coats. Sable. Chinchilla. They'll make a coat out of you once you fall into their clutches.'

'I don't care. She loves me.' Fracassus no sooner said it than even he knew it sounded wrong.

The Grand Duke shook his head as though he wanted never to see the world stationary again. 'When I think who you could have had last night,' he said at last.

The Grand Duchess looked away.

'They were students working as prostitutes,' Fracassus said. 'It's the only way they can afford to study the constitution.'

The Grand Duke turned the colour of the atrium at the Nowhere Palace. 'Studying the constitution! Miss North Pole! The runner-up to Miss Equator! Estrelita the supermodel! Yada-Yada, twice Playgirl of the Year! Mandarina, ex-mistress of three Formula 1 world champions! Need I go on? Why would women of that calibre be studying the constitution? Did you see the extension of their limbs? Did you see their elevation? You had the world to choose from and now you have nothing.'

'It's a club for hookers, Dad.'

'Wash your mouth out, boy. I met your mother there.'

Fracassus crept out in the night to revisit his father's club. Sojjourner? No Sojjourner had ever worked here. Had he made her up?

He requested that they let him into the cloakroom where he'd first talked to her, fantasy or not. He wanted to sit where she'd sat. Sniff the coats.

Gradually, one or two of the serving staff admitted they remembered her. He asked them if they knew anything about her being a Metropolitan Elitist. Some said they'd had their suspicions, others shrugged. In a club like this all deviances were respected.

A couple of prostitutes accosted him on the way in, and three more on the way out. He didn't have the heart for it, he told them. He'd lost his to a classy lady. So weren't they classy enough for him? He looked them up and down. They went a long way up. Yes, they were. But classy in a different way. He said he knew they needed money to continue their studies and offered them jobs at his new casino. They wondered when they'd be able to start. First I've got to build it, he told them. To ease their disappointment he made a grab at each of them in turn. He knew they wouldn't do him for assault. They wanted a job at his casino too much.

He resorted to Twitter. **Met a bitch called two js. Great piece of ass with two as. Moved on her, not close.**

But no tweet came back.

Aware that his son was not going to take silence for an answer and was preparing a Twitter blitz on Sojjourner's heart, the Grand Duke finally did what his wife had been asking him to do for years, and pulled the plug.

The building went out with a sigh.

'Listen to the silence,' the Grand Duchess exclaimed. 'Isn't it beautiful? No more bleeps and pings, no more chimes and quacks. No more clicks. No more hums. No more flashing blue lights that made our Palace resemble a police station.'

Fracassus grew irate. He raged up and down the building trying to get animation out of a television. He put his fist through one, but that didn't wake it. His phone was dead. Every keyboard unresponsive. He could neither receive a syllable nor send one.

This is a living hell, he thought.

But it gave him new entitlements.

He slipped out of the Palace in the middle of the day and visited the coffee shops he'd been barred from entering. There, his smartphone worked again. There, dunking ginger biscuits into frappucino, he tweeted again of the agonies of unrequited love. **You'll be sorry.**

If she was, she didn't say so.

Fuck, nigger, cunt, he was about to tweet, but the broadband dropped out at just that moment.

He went into a decline. He lost weight. He stopped totting up how much property he owned and how much he was worth. He stopped tweeting. **I am stopping tweeting**, he tweeted. He made a nuisance of himself with women in the Palace who found it difficult to rebuff him. He groped secretaries and grabbed cleaning staff. Some of them remembered he'd done the same to them when he was an infant. Same stubby little fingers. The Palace sommelier asked him what he had against intercourse – not that she was offering. He said he didn't think that he would like it. She told him she didn't think she liked being grabbed between the legs. Yeah you do, he said. Every woman likes being grabbed between the legs. She visited a lawyer who advised her to let sleeping dogs lie.

Dr Cobalt, now teaching the Prince the principles of governance, swore she saw a tear running down his cheek when she mentioned Foucault. A dry tear, if there were such a thing.

'I think there is,' Professor Probrius opined. He believed he'd read an ancient treatise somewhere on the constituent parts of tears. A tear of grief was wet and warm. A tear of compassion was wet and light. A tear of pique was dry and heavy and had no temperature.

'You're an unforgiving critic,' Dr Cobalt said.

'I'm hopeful, that's all. Pique is a quality not to be underestimated in the making of fools and tyrants.'

'And which do you think he will be?'

'The mistake is to think it has to be one or the other.'

There is a time-honoured method among the rich for dealing with a lovesick young man and healing his broken heart. You send him away.

BOOK TWO

There is no such thing as the will of the people. There is only the will of those who tell the people what the people's will should be.

Kolskeggur Probrius: *Phonoethics: A Manual* (Unpubl.)

CHAPTER 16

Containing the whole science of government

Great as was the consternation, and deep as was the sorrow in every heart, the moment for the Prince to leave came around without mishap or interference by the fates. Fracassus did nothing further untoward. And Sojjourner did not make a last-minute appearance. It was written. The world was waiting and it was time he ran into its embrace.

Professor Probrius and Dr Cobalt would accompany him, acting as mentors, confidants, travel guides and porters to the Prince and as eyes and ears to his parents. Report your every perturbation, they were told. But do not scruple to describe the highlights too.

Speaking for themselves, Professor Probrius and Dr Cobalt were delighted to be going. They too believed that indiscretions were best committed far from home.

The Grand Duke found it as hard as he knew it would be to bring the Grand Duchess round to Fracassus's departure. He reminded her that they had often been away and left their son, but accepted that this was different. When they had gone travelling the boy was safely ensconced in the Palace with a television to watch in every room; now he would be wandering God knows where. Not without technology – to compensate for his cruel pulling of the plug, the Grand Duke lavished the latest phones and tablets and laptops on Fracassus; even a watch that would double as a direct video link to the Palace and fitness activity tracker – though you could never be sure how good the signals were going to be in foreign parts. But he had mature company. And there were signs that he was maturing himself, if one only knew where to look for them. He'd been seasoned by misfortune. He had taken up tweeting again and had more than a million avid followers.

The Grand Duke and Duchess decided against going to the heliport, fearing the parting would prove emotional They saw the party off at the Golden Gates. Renzo took his son in his arms and begged him in a voice thick with emotion to remember all the advice he'd given him over the years. He had a great future. All he had to do now was earn it. Look, listen, learn. Limp and unresponsive, Fracassus gave the impression of somebody who'd forgotten everything that had ever been said to him already. 'Write to me,' his mother said, catching Probrius and Cobalt exchanging ironic looks. 'And I mean write, not tweet. I refuse to read those things.'

Wherever possible, Fracassus would travel first class, his tutors economy. This suited all parties. For their part, Professor Probrius and Dr Cobalt were pleased to have time together. They took that very particular pleasure in one another's company reserved for people who look alike. Both had attenuated bodies and long necks, both were pared down into that leanness often found among servants of the wealthy, and both had complementary sideways tilts that came from having to whisper into each other's ears in the presence of majesty. Thus they always looked hugger-mugger even when they weren't. Just what their travelling relations would be had not yet been decided. They would leave it, they thought, as they had left it for the last few years, to chance and opportunity. They weren't young and reckless like the Prince. They could wait. To tell the truth, they found postponement titillating.

Fracassus, who had yet to meet anyone his own age he resembled, had only himself for company. He didn't mind that. He had always preferred his own presence to that of other people. Moving from television set to television set in the weeks his parents were away, he had been free to let his mind riot in future scenarios of power. Solitude, he discovered, particularly when passed in front of a television screen, could be phantasmagoric. There had been times when what was true and what was not were so hard to tell apart that Fracassus felt he was exercising power already. 'Me,' he would cry inwardly, and sometimes even outwardly, as Nero lowered his thumb and the bodies piled up in the Colosseum. 'Me,' he would proclaim – *'Ich!'* – with every rewind of Max Schmeling flooring the Brown Bomber. Wrestlers, of course, were him. 'Do you submit now?' They didn't just submit, they whimpered their surrender. And feral motorists. Leaping from the burning car and watching it explode on the outskirts of the Mexican village, he felt a passing twinge of something – pride, was it? – knowing the other passengers had not been so fleet of foot and quick of thought. 'Me, me!' Their own fault if they were burnt alive or scarred irremediably. A mariachi band played to show there were no hard feelings. The car had been worth half a million in whatever currency.

Well, 'me' was a trickier entity after meeting Sojjourner. Sojjourner, who'd loitered briefly in his thoughts like a scented candle (his own simile) and then went out. For that brief time 'me' had become 'us'. But here he was, back to being singular again. He was surprised how quickly he'd got over the heartache and liked what it said about him. He was a tough guy. He was hurt-proof. **Love is for pussies**, he tweeted.

Though the helicopter flight to Gnossia was only half an hour – no more than a quick hop over the Wall – it irritated Fracassus that he had to travel the same class as everyone else. 'Can I sit on my own if I buy the airline?' he asked the pilot. 'That's not my decision, sir,' the pilot told him. Retard, Fracassus thought.

A delegation of Gnossian Republicans greeted Fracassus and his party on their arrival. Though Gnossia and Urbs-Ludus were essentially the same country divided by a Wall, the air felt different to Fracassus. Professor Probrius pointed out that this was because there were fewer towers and ziggurats in Gnossia, so they could see the sky. Fracassus seemed disgusted by the idea of fewer towers and wondered why they'd come to such a hellhole. 'Diplomacy, Your Highness,' Probrius reminded him. 'There has been tension between the two Republics. We are here to further your education, but let us not forget that this is, inter alia, a peace mission. The Grand Duke harbours high hopes for this visit. He believes you to have good negotiating skills.'

'I have great negotiating skills.'

'And that is why you're here.'

'Are these good hombres?' he asked Probrius, sotto voce.

'Very good.'

'Then tell them we want peace. And tell them if they want a few more towers I'll build them.'

'It would sound weightier coming from you, Your Royal Highness.'

A small dinner of fish that Fracassus refused to eat was thrown in honour of the visiting party, after which the Prince was granted an audience – though he hadn't asked for it – with the President of the Gnossian Republic, Eugenus Phonocrates. The President was elderly, and received Fracassus in his bed at the Presidential Palace. The President's face was lined as though he had been sleeping on a crumpled pillow all his life. He was said to have kind eyes but Fracassus, who was said to have no eyes, couldn't locate them in the great railway intersection of deep wrinkles.

'I once met your father,' Phonocrates said. 'He must have told you that. It's some years since we met but I see the family likeness in you.'

'I have his hair,' Fracassus said.

'And I hope his good character.'

'I have a great character,' Fracassus said.

Phonocrates tried to sit up in bed and called Fracassus closer to him. It didn't occur to Fracassus to offer help. 'Many years ago,' Phonocrates said, 'your father told me he admired the way I ran my country and asked me to divulge to him the secret of good government. I told him that if he would ever do me the honour of sending his son to meet me, I would divulge it to him. You have an older brother, I believe. He never did come to see me. I don't know why.' (Transgender faggot, Fracassus decided against telling him.) 'So I am doubly honoured that you have.'

Fracassus inclined his head. The President waited for him to say the honour was all his, but he didn't say it.

'Anyway,' the President continued, 'I am today pleased to be keeping my promise. That is not something I usually do . . .' He paused, coughed, and banged his chest. 'And there you have it.'

Fracassus waited. 'There I have what?' he asked at last.

'The whole secret of good government.'

'Where? What?'

'Don't keep your promises.'

Fracassus had no idealism to be outraged, but even he was taken aback by the old man's candour.

'Not any?'

'Not any . . . I know what you are thinking. I might have got away with not keeping *some* of my promises. But *all*! And maybe for a short time. But for more than *sixty years*! But this is to miss the point. And listen to me carefully now . . . To be successful in politics you must be thorough. If you are half-hearted you will fail. A half-hearted liar the people will not forgive. "Ah!" they will say, "did you hear that, did you notice that? He has just told a lie. He cannot be trusted." But if they know you to be a liar through and through, and you show that you know they know you to be a liar, they can trust you. They grow fond of your lies. Eventually they will come to feel that the lies you tell are their lies. It is like pillow talk. Everyone lies in love. That's the game. You don't honestly believe what you say to one another. She is not really the most beautiful woman on the planet, and you are not really the most handsome man. But in the game of love you pretend it is so and think none the less of one another for telling lies and believing them. The game of politics is the same. *Tomorrow you will all be employed* – you promise. *The day after tomorrow you will all have free healthcare. The day after that you will pay no taxes.* Who really believes any of that is going to happen? Not the people, much as they would like to. And while they love me for telling them what they want to hear, they love me even more for the theatre of illusion I give them. They think I am the villain in a pantomime and everybody cheers the villain in a pantomime. You ask me are the people stupid. Very far from it. They can smell a fraud a thousand miles away. But ask me if they know what's best for them, then the answer is a resounding no, because their besetting weakness is that they love a fraudster. If someone who wants the best for the people lets them down, they will never forgive him. But a joker who wants the worst for them they will follow into hell – this, Prince Fracassus, is what I would have told your father.'

The following morning, Eugenus Phonocrates, lover of the people, was found dead in his bed.

No one blamed Fracassus.

He stayed for the state funeral. Bells rang. Hundreds of thousands of people lined the streets. Men and women of all ages wept openly. Some cut their arms and faces. Any baby born that day, no matter what the sex, was named Eugenus Phonocrates.

At the biggest sporting arena a football match was called off so a memorial service could be held. Fracassus, as heir presumptive to the Duchy of Origen, was guest of honour. He sat between Phonocrates' sons on a raised platform in the centre of the field, carried a candle, thought of Sojjourner in her trousers and wept a hard dry tear for the cameras.

Midway through the service, by which time the mourning had fed on itself like a flame, leaping from the mourners' chests as though to be consumed by their own fervour was the only end they sought, a wild person wearing rags broke though the crowds and dropped at Fracassus's feet. Carried away by the emotion sweeping through the stadium, the security services did nothing to remove the intruder. He was part of it. His own private conflagration.

Fracassus did what he always did when he was afraid and jutted his jaw.

'Listen to them,' the wild man said, as though to someone sitting on the Prince's shoulder. 'Behold the wondrousness of human folly.'

'I don't frighten easily,' Fracassus said. 'I have less fear than any man on the planet.'

The wild man ignored his words. 'Look around you,' he went on. 'Man in his massed magnificence. Crowds screamed and cried for me once. Women said and did disgusting things. They encouraged their own daughters to do the same. They abandoned shame, if they had ever known it. I was the best-known singer in Gnossia. The Republic came to a halt when I sang. The radio fell silent. Doctors stopped performing operations. Tickets for my concerts changed hands for more than people paid for their houses. I loved the crazed attention. I studied every face. I drank in the adulation of every person in that crowd. I had the power not just to move but to possess. They weren't listening to my voice, they *were* my voice. I loved it and then I hated it. I had thought it was about me but it wasn't. It was about them. They screamed because they needed to scream. They waved their arms in the air like one great beast with a thousand limbs because they wanted to lose their humanity. That was the only way they could find themselves – by losing what made them separate. Singing, dancing, marching, sport, religion, mourning, war – they're all the same when the great beast waves its million arms. Only by losing do they find. Something must have happened in the history of humanity that made people cast away their reason. Maybe it was the appearance of a strange planet. Maybe God descended. Maybe it was the applause humanity awarded itself when it moved in a mass out of the great soup of creation. "We've made it! We've done it! We're here!" Whatever the cause, adulation for themselves in the appearance of another became a fixture of human life. You no doubt think that when you are applauded it's because of something you have said, or done, or just because of the way you look. Disabuse yourself. You simply fill a vacuum. The need for you, whoever you are, was there long before you were. You are the object of the habit of hysteria, that's all.'

Fracassus felt himself sliding into a trance. They can't half talk, these Gnossians, he thought. Then, through half-closed eyes, he saw the once famous singer raise his hand. He's going to kill me, Fracassus thought. It's me he blames. He remembered Max Schmeling and made a fist. Then he landed it in the middle of the singer's face.

Reports at once spread that as part of a well-orchestrated coup there'd been an attempt on the lives of Phonocrates' grieving sons. Prince Fracassus, son of the Grand Duke of Origen, here from the Republic of Urbs-Ludus on a peace mission, had foiled it. Cheers mingled with tears. The habit of hysteria had gone looking for a cause and found it in Fracassus.

Back in the Palace of the Golden Gates, watching the late news on television, the Grand Duke saw it happen. He would have liked to call his wife but she was locked away in her fairy-grotto chocolate factory. 'My boy!' the Grand Duke said, alone.

Fracassus gave interviews to the world's press gathered in Gnossia to report on Phonocrates' funeral. The late President was a great guy, he said. He shook his head and, with a dying fall, repeated the felicitous phrase. 'Great guy . . . great guy . . .'

Had he been frightened? No, he had no fear, no fear.

Anything else?

He raised his face to the cameras. 'It's been a great night, thank you, thank you.' Then he remembered a line Professor Probrius had given him for a rainy day. 'The fight against terror goes on.'

CHAPTER 17

A hero of our time

There being nothing further to keep them in Gnossia, the Prince's party betook themselves to the little airport. Fracassus didn't like flying but at least he had a row of first-class seats to himself. He settled in to watching television on the back of someone else's seat in a tongue he didn't recognise on a screen the size of a postage stamp.

Language had never been an insuperable barrier to Fracassus's enjoyment of anything. The conversations he most enjoyed were the ones he couldn't hear or understand and even his favourite television programmes worked best for him with the sound turned off so he could interpolate his own dialogue. Some people's brains are crammed and noisy places; Fracassus – though he enjoyed commotion and liked imagining himself to be its cause – kept a quiet head. The word 'me' pinged about in it like a bagatelle ball in a deserted basilica.

And now 'me' was an entity they had tried to kill and failed. The word suggested impregnability. 'Me' was armour plating.

Soon after the plane took off, he found himself engrossed in a game show, the essentials of which would have been plain in any tongue. Based loosely on a sketch by a once beloved foreign comedian called Monty Python – repeats of which Fracassus had watched a hundred times without finding them remotely funny, so there must have been nothing else on those nights – the show comprised a host wearing a faceted metallic suit, a hostess exiguously dressed in banknotes, a studio audience exceptionally collaborative in spirit, and the contestants themselves, tempted to blow the whistle on people they loved, whether by giving away their secrets to their spouses, divulging their medical histories, casting doubts on their legitimacy, or informing on them to the police. The longer they held out against betrayal, the plumper the brown paper envelope they were offered, though of course – or there would have been no point to the game – the offer might be rescinded at any time. You had to choose your moment. Those who refused to stab their friends in the back were jeered – 'Spravnos,' the studio audience called out, which Fracassus translated as 'Lock 'em up!' – while those who held out for more money and then sold their family down the river were applauded wildly. 'Spravchik,' the audience shouted, which Fracassus took to mean 'We love you.' Fracassus registered a provisional interest in the witch-queen hostess, part Lilith, part Shinigami, who handed out or held back the envelopes, dropping a curtsy either way, in order to avoid bending over. But it was the Tempter in Chief himself, brawny as a bear but soft-voiced like a serpent, who grabbed Fracassus's attention. 'Me,' Fracassus thought, as the plane landed at Cholm airport.

A middlingly-stretch limousine was waiting to collect the party and transport them to their hotel. The cocktail cabinet and television were smaller than his father's but Fracassus was, for him, too full of what he'd been watching on the flight to complain. 'So what exactly was the principle of this game?' Dr Cobalt asked. She would have liked to take in the scenery of a country she had never visited before, but this was not a journey for her pleasure. And besides, flushed from whatever had happened in Gnossia, Fracassus had turned voluble and peremptory.

'You get money for shopping your friends,' he explained. Already he had assumed the menacingly soft tones of the Master of Betrayal.

'Is that it?'

'And people shout "spravchik".'

'Spravchik?'

'Spravchik.'

On hearing this word, the driver of the limousine swung round in his seat. 'You know Spravchik?'

Dr Cobalt looked at Professor Probrius. They were both accomplished linguists, but no, neither of them knew what spravchik was.

'Spravchik is not a what, he's a who,' the driver called over his shoulder. 'Vozzek Spravchik is our Foreign Secretary.'

'Why, in that case, would people have been calling out his name on a game show?' Probrius asked.

'Why? Why not? It's his show. They were calling for him.' *Cheem, they were calling for cheem*, he pronounced to the Prince's delight. Setting aside Gnossia, where people spoke the same language he spoke, Fracassus had never left Urbs-Ludus and had not heard a foreign accent before. His genius for mimicry was tickled. *Cheem*, he kept saying to himself. He added it to his repertoire. Lordy, lordy; the floppy-limbed spastic bedmaker, and now *cheem*. A comic routine was taking shape.

Probrius did know something of the world beyond the Republic, but he was still surprised by what the driver told him. 'Your Foreign Secretary is a game-show host? Is there not a conflict of interests?'

'What conflict? He is also Minister of Home Affairs, and Culture Secretary. Why not? No conflict.' *Confleect.*

A thrill went through Fracassus. *Confleect. Chwy not. Cheem.* Life had become very amusing suddenly. If only he had an audience bigger than Probrius and Cobalt to amuse. An audience the size of the one that had watched him knock out the subversive singer. *Spravchik*!

The next day, following a morning of sightseeing in which Fracassus saw nothing, Vozzek Spravchik invited the Prince and his little party to meet him at the Ministry. The plan before they'd left home had been for Fracassus to travel this leg of the journey incognito, without the hindrance of diplomatic nicety and protocol, but he had been so insistent in his desire to see the Minister in the flesh, that messages had been hurriedly exchanged, permissions sought, and here they were.

To Fracassus's disappointment, the Minister greeted them in an ordinary lounge suit and without his assistant from the show. He could have been a civil servant. But then he took his tie off and spiny black bristling hairs, that reminded Fracassus of a wild boar he'd seen on a natural history programme, sprang from his shirt. A pungent smell came off him. On the walls of his office were photographs of Spravchik in his swimming trunks, driving a jeep, diving, surfing and standing in an Olympic pool balancing on each shoulder the two synchronised swimmers who'd won silver medals for their country in the recent games. There were also two life-size paintings in the heroic style – one of him arm-wrestling a polar bear and the other of him gently removing a thorn from a lion's paw. 'These are the two sides to my personality,' he explained. Fracassus's initial disappointment in the man dissolved in his admiration for the art.

'Welcome, anyway, to you all,' Spravchik proclaimed, as though to a vast gathering, extending a hand to each of the party in turn. 'There are, I hope, no hard feelings left between our peoples. Sometimes you have to have enemies to know who your friends are.'

Though Fracassus was not aware there'd been hard feelings between the Republic of Urbs-Ludus and Cholm, he liked Spravchik's verbal style and wanted to show he could match it. 'And sometimes you have to be right to be wrong,' he responded.

Spravchik appeared delighted by this and clasped Fracassus to his strong chest. 'We should wrestle,' he said.

Professor Probrius wasn't sure that was a good idea. The Prince had only recently got off a long-haul flight and was no doubt suffering jet lag.

'And I have just knocked someone out with my fist,' Fracassus added.

The Minister roared his approval. 'Show me how you did it.'

'Not a good idea,' Probrius put in, fearing another diplomatic incident. 'Perhaps in a few days, when the Prince is recovered, Minister.'

'Just name the day. That will be beautiful. I have a full-size wrestling ring.'

'That is an occasion we all look forward to,' said Dr Cobalt.

'Looking forward can be dangerous,' said Spravchik, 'but not as dangerous as looking back.'

Fracassus decided against trying to match his verbal style again. 'How long have you been doing your show?' he enquired instead.

'Is a question I am always asked: which came first, your political career or show business? Chicken/egg, egg/chicken. I say they came together. What's the difference? The people love my show and vote for me. The people vote for me then watch my show. Trust the people. They don't make the false divisions intellectuals do. Whoever touches the soul of the people embraces truth. The people sometimes need guidance but they are never wrong. The people are beautiful. You want tickets?'

Probrius and Cobalt were about to shake their heads but Fracassus nodded his.

'We are recording this evening. You must come. All of you. I will get you tickets. Never put off doing until tomorrow what you can do today – and that includes invading your neighbours . . .' He paused to measure his effect. 'Only having fun with you,' he went on.

'Sometimes fun can be mistress to a not-so-funny deed,' Professor Probrius said, though the moment he said it he couldn't understand why he had.

Nor could Minister Spravchik. He narrowed his eyes and showed his teeth, much as he did when offering a contestant money to betray his best friend's political affiliations to the secret police. Professor Probrius started from the steely light. Fracassus felt drawn into it. This was the first great man he had ever encountered face to face. Compared to Spravchik, Philander and Hopsack were minnows. And Eugenus Phonocrates was dead. 'Yes, please,' he said. He had a new word and wondered if he had the courage to use it. 'Tickets would be beautiful.'

'It takes great faith to ask,' the Minister said, clasping Fracassus to him again. 'And it takes even greater faith to give. I am guided by my faith in everything I do. I have so much faith in me you can hear it beating against my ribs. No man has more faith.'

Fracassus listened and could hear it. He had promised his mother he would write and now he knew what he would say. 'Dear Mother, I have just held genius in my arms. Don't worry. Not a Rationalist Progressivist. Not a hooker either. Your loving son, Fracassus.'

That night he sat in the front row of *Whistle-Blowers* and when the crowd rose to bait the faint of heart, so did he. 'Spravnos!' he shouted.

Professor Probrius also planned his email to his employers. 'We have barely been away three days but already Fracassus has won the hearts of all Gnossians, and is now further extending his understanding of foreign customs,' he would write. 'He is winning friends and forging new alliances wherever we go. The honour he is lending to the name of Origen is all you would have wished for.'

Lying in Yoni Cobalt's arms he whispered, 'Spravchik.'

The Doctor jumped up. Many were the hours and long were the nights through which she'd lain in a fever of desire, imagining just such a moment as this – she and Kolskeggur alone in a foreign place, listening to the howling of the wolves, far from television and the Internet, every minute before dawn theirs to do with as they wanted. And he had chosen to whisper 'Spravchik' in her ear. What did he mean by it? Was he playing some perverted jealousy game? Was he one of those men who needed to feel rejected before he could feel loved? 'I'm not turned on by Spravchik if that's what you're trying to find out,' she said.

'I should hope you're not,' Probrius said. 'Neither am I. But it would appear our little Prince is. For a supposed tough guy he's easily swayed by other tough guys, wouldn't you say?'

'What are you implying?'

Professor Probrius laughed. He didn't know. That the boy was dangerously susceptible to muscularity, that was all.

Yoni Cobalt saw it as the Prince trying out what sort of man to be. He'd been groomed to greatness. But what kind of greatness? It was up to them, wasn't it, to show him other ways than Spravchik.

Kolskeggur Probrius kissed her fondly. 'You want to make a good man of him, do you? Who are your models? Jesus? Gandhi? Doesn't he own too much property to make it into their league? You can't grow up on a Monopoly board and hope to direct others how to live nobly.'

'You can if you discard the Monopoly board.'

'And the television.'

'Yes, and the television.'

'And the Internet.'

'Yes and the Internet.'

'And the social media.'

'Yes, definitely the social media.'

'And then there's abnegation of the ego.'

'So we'll leave him to Spravchik, then?'

They went to sleep thinking their own thoughts. Not for the first time, Probrius felt that if he could only stay patient things would work out nicely in his favour. Fracassus a saviour? Hardly. Fracassus a scourge, more like.

He listened to what the wind was saying, and it agreed with him.

Minister Spravchik would not hear of Fracassus and his party leaving just yet. He put a super-stretch government limo at their disposal, together with an interpreter and a guide to the country's monuments and museums. Just as the car was about to pull away he ran out in front of it, waved it down, and jumped inside. He was wearing a track-suit in the colours of his country and a bobble skiing hat. 'You two can get lost,' he told the interpreter and the guide, pointing his thumbs back over his shoulder.

Fracassus added another expression to his collection. *You two can get lost.* And then the thumbs. He'd use that one day.

'What I think we'll do first,' Minister Spravchik told them, pouring himself a slivovitz from the limo's cocktail cabinet and knocking it back in one swallow, 'is go up into the Blackbread Mountains where you will be able to see indigenous handicrafts being made and taste the local brew. Then if there's time we'll go back down into the White Canyon and do the same.'

He foamed with laughter, which Fracassus reciprocated.

The colour went out of Spravchik's face. 'The idea of meeting indigenous people amuses you?'

'No,' Fracassus said. All the colour that had fled Spravchik's face flew into his. 'I thought it amused you.'

'Why would it amuse me? I am Culture Secretary. The welfare of our most ancient and poorest inhabitants is of the first importance to me.'

They drove into the mountains in silence. Fracassus had never been into mountains before. But he couldn't look around him. He was too upset.

Spravchik's mood, however, appeared to improve. 'Come,' he said, when the car stopped at the summit. 'First we enjoy the view – the greatest in the world. Then we watch the ceremony of the threading of the beads. People have been practising the art of bead threading on this very spot for hundreds of thousands of years. They mine the quartz from the mountain, shape them with flint stones, drill holes through them with a sharpened dogwood stick which they rub between their hands – a method unique to Cholm – then string them on ropes made from the wild vine liana. Come. Look.'

Sitting outside a rough habitation were a dozen of the saddest, blackest individuals Fracassus had ever seen. They appeared to have been staring vacantly into space until the party wandered over, whereupon they bent their heads industriously and began the drilling.

'It must hurt their hands to do that,' Fracassus said. He wanted to show what a great interest he was taking in the indigenous customs of Spravchik's country.

'Not any more,' Spravchik said. 'They were doing this when you were still a bacterium in the belly of a wriggle fish. Here' – he seized a finished necklace of beads from a woven basket and hung it around the Prince's neck – 'a gift from the Numa people. Now we'll go over to witness the fermentation ceremony and have a drink.'

Fracassus fingered the beads and got immediately drunk.

'Strong, huh?' Spravchik said, enfolding Fracassus in his arms.

'You?'

'The drink. We'll make a man of you before you leave us . . . Unless I can persuade you to stay. Will you?' (It was the same low serpent hiss Spravchik used to persuade contestants to sell their sisters for sixpence.) 'Say yes. We could invade a country together. I'll let you pick one. What do you say, Professor Probrius? Can I have him? And you, Dr Cobalt? Your role is the mother's, I presume. Can you bear to part with him?'

There was much mirth and saying 'If only', but it was impossible to know if the invitation was genuine.

On the road down from the mountain Spravchik continued to enthuse about the Numa people and their customs. But the moment they were back on flat land he began to inveigh against their laziness, their alcoholism, the tawdriness of what he called 'their shitty little customs', and the cost to the exchequer of keeping them in welfare.

The party fell quiet. Fracassus because he was asleep, Professor Probrius and Dr Cobalt because of who they were.

'I know what you are thinking,' Spravchik said to Dr Cobalt whom he had picked from the start as subversively liberal.

'I'm not thinking anything, Minister, except how beautiful your country is.'

'I appreciate your flattery but I know your culture and I know you are wondering how I can praise the peasants when I am among them and wish to exterminate them when I am not.'

'I hadn't thought you wished to exterminate them, Minister,' Dr Cobalt said.

'There you are. That's the very judgementalism I was referring to. Exterminate is just a manner of speaking. I could as easily have said "remove" or "relocate", but I wanted to provoke you into outrage. And I have succeeded. Allow me to say that you don't appreciate the complexity of holding several conflicting portfolios simultaneously. I have to be all things to all people in this country. On the mountain I am Culture Secretary. Down here I am Minister for Home Affairs.'

Fracassus had woken up. 'And you are beautiful as both,' he said, slurring his speech.

As was the custom in Cholm, Minister Spravchik kissed him on the mouth.

CHAPTER 18

In which Fracassus almost reads a book

Picture the emotions warring in the chest of young Fracassus. Word of his fame as the hero of Gnossia reached him intermittently. Cholm was mountainous and the signal erratic. He tweeted his thanks to his admirers but couldn't be sure they ever reached them. This was the wrong place to be at such a time. It was as though the world was celebrating his birthday without him. But didn't Spravchik's company compensate for this? He wasn't sure whether to be flattered by Spravchik's friendship or miffed that Spravchik wasn't adequately flattered by his. Did Spravchik always mean what he said? Where, for example, was the promised wrestle?

But the most perplexing question of all concerned heroism. Could one be a hero *and* a hero-worshipper?

To the best of anyone's knowledge, that's to say to the best of his own knowledge, Fracassus didn't dream, but he was getting perilously close to dreaming of Vozzek Spravchik. He felt spurred to emulation but somehow diminished at the same time. Was heroism a virtue one could forfeit in the act of admiring it in others? He would have liked to discuss this with his father, but his father was far away. This left only Professor Probrius, whom he didn't like and after more than half a dozen words couldn't follow, and Dr Cobalt, but Dr Cobalt was a woman. Could a man – *should* a man – discuss heroism with a member of the very sex heroism existed to impress?

He decided he would raise the matter with her casually, much as he might raise the matter of a missing shirt. Just by the by, did she happen to know of any blog or vlog or YouTube video on the subject of heroism? She wondered why he wanted it. She ventured to hope he hadn't gone overboard on Spravchik.

'Overboard?'

'Well, he is what many would regard as a heroic figure and I can see that you respect him.'

'What's wrong with that?'

'There's nothing wrong with respecting any man so long as he is worthy of it.'

'And you think Spravchik isn't? Is that because he drinks?'

'Not just that. The man has an appalling human rights record.'

'Because he arm-wrestles bears?'

'No, I wouldn't call arm-wrestling a bear a violation of human rights. Though it might violate animal rights.'

'What if the bear wins?'

'Good for the bear, but the gay and lesbian people he imprisons and the women he flogs for having abortions won't be consoled by that.'

Fracassus allowed his mouth to fall open. There was an unwritten code at the Palace as to what did and did not constitute appropriate conversation between a prince and his tutor. There were grey areas but abortion wasn't one of them. As for any sexualities other than heterosexuality, no mention was permitted of these either after Jago's dereliction. Had foreign travel caused Dr Cobalt to forget herself?

She asked herself the same question. 'I apologise if I have offended you, Your Highness,' she said. 'I thought you were asking my opinion.'

'*Your* opinion! When I want an opinion I ask a man.'

'In that case might I suggest Bear Grylls' *Spirit of the Jungle*. I'm told it's a stirring adventure story.'

Story! Fracassus shook his head in frustration. *Spirit of the Jungle* sounded like the stuff his mother had tried to force on him. Spirits, fairies, fantastic beasts. What would Spravchik think of him reading a *story* about animals you couldn't wrestle because they weren't really there? He pushed his face out at her. 'I don't want fake-fiction,' he shouted.

Dr Cobalt turned pale. 'I will think about it further,' she said. Later that day she arranged for Nietzsche's *Thus Spoke Zarathustra* and Thomas Carlyle's *On Heroes, Hero-Worship and the Heroic in History* to be delivered to the Prince electronically and waited for what he would have to say to her about them.

In the meantime she wondered if she'd gone too far and would be recalled to Urbs-Ludus. She told Kolskeggur what she'd done.

'You brought up the matter of Spravchik's violations of human rights with the Prince?'

She screwed her eyes up. 'Have I been a fool?'

'What did Fracassus think?'

'Fracassus doesn't think. He looked ill-pleased.'

'By you, or by Spravchik's violations?'

'I very much doubt the latter. He has grown up in a jungle of human rights violations.'

'Tut, tut.'

'Are you tutting me or the Grand Duke?'

He kissed her forehead. A fatherly kiss. 'I'll tell you what I think,' he said. 'Whenever I heard people talking about human rights in my university I wanted to reach for my shotgun.'

'Kolskeggur!'

'That wasn't because I wanted anything less for the despised and underprivileged than they did. I just described my outrage differently.'

'Thereby making it about yourself.'

'No, the very opposite.'

'Are you saying I was making Spravchik's crimes about me?'

'That depends on what exactly you said and how you said it. But if you flew the flag of your emotions and showed your pain, then yes.'

'Human rights are a flag to you?'

'They will be to Fracassus. The very phrase affects members of his class the way a spade affects a garden worm. They might not be able to describe the weapon but they know they're under attack from it.'

'Silence is a recipe for defeatism.'

'Whatever war you're fighting you already aren't winning. Listen to what's in the wind. May I speak my mind?'

'Well, it would appear I have spoken mine.'

Professor Probrius took a breath. Never a good sign if you were the interlocutor. 'Every time you champion a special interest group you alienate those who fall outside it. That does make them illiberal. I don't say be silent but I do say clean up your language. Change your precious cast of victims. Don't make an enemy of anyone who doesn't feel the hurt you do. Or just don't give a damn.'

Dr Cobalt didn't know why she suddenly felt peeved, but she did.

'Do you know what?' she said. 'Why don't you talk to the little prick your way and I'll talk to him mine?'

Professor Probrius put up a hand of peace. Her way would work out perfectly nicely for him. She might as well have been loading Fracassus up with sticks of dynamite. He didn't want any harm to come to her. He hoped that if he listened to the wind he would know when the explosion was coming and would be able to whisk her away from it. But that didn't mean he wasn't looking forward to the bang.

Fracassus said nothing further to Dr Cobalt that day. She couldn't tell what mood he was in with her. But he did leave his PlayWatch lying about – perhaps deliberately – and she noticed what he was reading on it. Bear Grylls' *The Spirit of the Jungle*, abridged.

CHAPTER 19

The spirit of the jungle

The party remained in the country of the Numa for several months, though there was no further trip to the mountains. Fracassus continued to receive tickets for Spravchik's television show and attended it religiously. On one evening the warm-up man's role was taken by Spravchik himself. 'Tonight you'll have to put up with me in all capacities,' he told the crowd who shouted and called his name. He must have been aware of Fracassus's presence because he translated some of his funny stories into a form Fracassus could understand.

Between anecdotes he talked about the deviancy that was eating the heart out of his country the way mice gnaw at a harvest. Homosexuality, he said, was against the will of God, whichever god you believed in. The Numa people, for example, before whose ancient wisdom he stood in awe, would throw any child showing homoerotic inclinations off the mountain. They could detect these inclinations in the first six months of the child's life. And the moment they did – he made a motion suggestive of spading dirt into an empty grave – it was over the side with them. There was no hatred in this; it was all kindness. They couldn't bear the thought of homosexual children going through life scarred by their unnaturalness.

'Spravchik!' the studio audience cried.

He had one more thing to say. For himself, he would rather have cancer than a lesbian for a daughter.

Spravchik! Spravchik!

Did he fling a smile – suggestive of spading dirt into an empty grave – at Fracassus?

Fracassus knew what he would tell Dr Cobalt should the subject of Spravchik's violations of human rights crop up again. He would tell her that Spravchik was motivated by kindness not cruelty. He would tell her the Minister was joking. And he would tell her to remember her place.

Some of the tweets Fracassus composed in the time he was Spravchik's guest throw light on his feelings for the man:

4 May: **Great meeting with Vozzek Spravchik, television host extraordinary and Culture Secretary of this great country.**

6 May: **Journey to mountains with Vozzek. Great view. The Numa present me with bead necklace. Lovely people.**

6 May: **Vozzek says country can't afford to go on looking after Numa people who drink too much. Sad.**

9 May: **Wrestle with Vozzek Spravchik, Minister of Home Affairs and Whistle-Blower host. I let him win.**

11 May: **Rematch. I let him win again.**

20 May: **Go swimming with Vozzek. Someone pulls my shorts off under water. Great guy.**

20 May: **Person who pulls my shorts off not Vozzek but I think his assistant from Whistle-Blower.**

29 May: **I'm learning so much here. Could stay forever.**

7 June: **Appalled to hear of violent demonstrations in my country. What do these people want . . .**

7 June: **. . . they have everything.**

8 June: **Vozzek offers to send army to restore order. Classy guy.**

17 June: **Vozzek Spravchik's daughter announces she is lesbian. So sad.**

Eager to mobilise his forces though Foreign Secretary and Defence Minister Spravchik was, he didn't again invite Fracassus to pick somewhere on the map for them to invade. Fracassus was disappointed. Had it all been just another tease? Nor did Spravchik send help to Urbs-Ludus where the troubles had apparently subsided as quickly as they'd begun. But he did say his country was constantly monitoring the situation and that Fracassus could rest assured that his parents were safe and calm. Fracassus thanked him for the reassurance but wondered how he came by his information. 'By hacking into your father's computer system,' Spravchik laughed.

Joking aside – supposing he were joking – something seemed to be troubling the Minister. He could not see Fracassus without embracing him and then withdrawing from his company with a sigh.

Not counting Sojjourner – and Fracassus was no longer counting Sojjourner – Fracassus had never been in love. So he didn't know the signs. When Nero was in love he showed his feelings by raping the girl's mother. But that didn't help Fracassus in his current predicament. Was Spravchik in love with him or not?

Finally, on a horse ride into the Makindo Desert – Fracassus sitting behind the bare-chested Spravchik and clasping him tentatively round the waist – the Minister unburdened himself of what had been on his mind. He wanted a casino. Something memorable and monumental. And he wanted Fracassus to design it.

Was that all? Fracassus was disappointed. He'd hoped . . . but what had he hoped?

Of course he said yes.

Delighted, Spravchik proposed they toe-wrestled. Cholm was the world capital of toe-wrestling and an invitation to toe-wrestle the Culture Secretary was the highest honour the country could bestow.

Spravchik rode them to a natural amphitheatre, where fallen logs served for seats and two rocks, the distance of two men apart, were positioned like pillows. Spravchik told Fracassus to strip down to his *Unterhosen*. Fracassus was embarrassed: his legs were fine but he rightly feared his pecs were flabby. Spravchik explained the rules. They would stretch their lengths upon the stony ground, lie right foot to right foot, then left foot to left foot, pillow their heads upon the rocks, interlock big toes, and attempt to force the other's foot into the flaming torches which Spravchik would now light. Best of seventeen throws. And damned be him that first cries 'Hold!' There would be no witnesses – Spravchik had a servant shave his chest, and then dismissed him.

They shook hands, then took up their positions. Fracassus looked up into the sky. Above him eagles soared. The sun beat down. 'Spravchik!' Spravchik shouted, and so it began. Their feet locked, their big toes, equally matched despite the difference in their years, clamped like spanners or the claws of eagles. Fracassus felt the strain of effort through his thighs and back. Spravchik hummed quietly to himself. The advantage went this way and that. Doubtful it stood, as two spent swimmers that do cling together.

The light began to dim.

And all day long the noise of battle rolled . . .

The following day, back in the Ministry, the two men, limping slightly, talked zoning and location.

'Build it wherever you like,' Spravchik said.

That was when Fracassus had his brainwave. 'Let's build it in the Blackbread Mountains,' he said.

Spravchik leapt from his chair and embraced him. Then he stepped back and tapped his lip.

Was he wondering what to do about the Numa, Fracassus enquired. If so, he had the perfect solution. They could work in the kitchens and thread beads in the foyer.

Spravchik embraced him again. 'Nice thought,' he said. 'But we must respect their ancient culture.'

Fracassus nodded. 'How do we do that?'

'We resettle them in some slum!'

Fracassus was relieved. He'd hoped Spravchik would see it that way.

He stayed on a year to see the project through its developmental stage. He tweeted links to artists' impressions of the building. **Classy partnership: classy building.** News of its construction travelled far and wide. The Pleasure Temple of Numa, the pillars of its sacrificial temple stretching high into the clouds.

Yoni Cobalt, in Kolskeggur Probrius's arms, wondered how long it would be before they'd be throwing babies who showed gay tendencies off its ramparts.

'Shh,' Kolskeggur Probrius said.

CHAPTER 20

Fracassus discovers the price of freedom and tweets about it

The party left Cholm by train. Fracassus was sad to leave. He felt that a part of himself would always remain here. He and Spravchik had embraced in private on the morning of departure. Fracassus liked to think that between men of surpassing power there existed a sort of electric force field and that when they embraced, especially for the final time, sparks like those emitted by the First Creation would fly between them. No such sparks flew between Spravchik and Fracassus, but it was a melancholy farewell notwithstanding.

Though the journey was reputed to be beautiful, Fracassus didn't notice the meadows or the streams. There was good coverage on the train and he didn't want to miss it. He was pleased to find his name wherever he looked and to see himself widely talked about. 'What's a wunderkind?' he asked Professor Probrius.

'A wonder child. Why?'

'That's what they're calling me.'

'That's what you are, Your Highness.'

Less satisfying was the news from Urbs-Ludus. More disturbances were reported. Every day another demonstration against something. Every demonstration lasting longer than the one before. He sent an email to his father in the language of Twitter which was now the only language he could think in. He hoped it would convey the seriousness of his concern. **Minister Spravchik sad to see me go. Everyone is. Even a wunderkind has to stay focussed.**

Probrius hadn't arranged for a car to meet them this time. He didn't want another Spravchik situation. Better to get their passports stamped and slip in otherwise unobserved. A little more fuss was made of Fracassus on account of his title than Probrius thought necessary, but sycophancy always put the boy in better temper. 'Welcome to Plasentza, Prince Fracassus.' When a stranger called him Prince it was as though he had never heard the word before and became a stranger to himself. He would stand around, waiting to collect every rag of accolade, before he could be persuaded to move on. The luggage was being sent on ahead so they could walk through the city. Fracassus rarely walked and had certainly never walked anywhere like this.

'What have your brought me to?' he asked as they left the station. He had noticed people sleeping on the floor. He guessed this was because their trains were late. But then he saw people sleeping in shop doorways as well.

'It's called an advanced liberal democracy,' Probrius explained.

'What does that mean?'

'It means there's no monarchy, no presidency and no dictatorship.'

'So who runs the place?'

'Elected members of parliament.'

'Who elects them?'

'The people.'

'Who elects the people?'

'No one elects the people. They're the people. They just are.'

Fracassus scratched his face.

'This,' Professor Probrius went on, 'is considered to be the fairest form of government mankind has yet devised.'

Fracassus pointed to a couple of beggars sleeping top to tail in a cardboard box in the doorway of a coffee shop. He asked if they were toe-wrestling. Professor Probrius said he didn't think so.

'Then why are they here?'

'Because there's nowhere else for them to sleep.'

'But aren't they the people?'

'You are indeed a wunderkind, Your Highness,' Professor Probrius said. 'You put your finger at once on the contradiction at the heart of government by the people. It doesn't work because people aren't nice to one another.'

'Just a minute . . .' Dr Cobalt began, but Professor Probrius stared her into silence.

'How,' Fracassus wondered, 'do you unelect the people?'

Dr Cobalt was again frozen into silent compliance by Probrius's stare.

'It's been tried, Your Highness. Your father has been wrongly accused of doing that very thing. A better way, in my view – and, if I may say so, in the view of many experts – is to give the people what they want in the full knowledge that they don't know and then let them give the power back to you.'

Dr Cobalt could contain herself no longer. 'Whereupon it will cease to be a liberal democracy,' she said.

'And whose fault will that be?' Professor Probrius asked.

Fracassus had the answer. 'The people's.'

'It's never a good idea,' Professor Probrius said, feeling he was coaching the Prince already, 'to tell the people you are saving them from themselves. Better to tell them you're saving them from someone else.'

'Like who?' Fracassus wondered.

'Like anyone you can come up with.'

Dr Cobalt's look met Professor Probrius's. *Like your father,* they were both thinking.

Fracassus had an identical thought.

The following morning a bomb went off not many streets from their hotel. Six people were killed. Dozens injured. Fracassus watched the news on the hotel television. He could smell sweet gunpowder. And something worse.

It was by no means the first time such a crime had been committed and innocent bystanders killed or wounded. 'This is the price we pay for our freedoms,' a senior politician was saying. He had been accused before of taking a sort of satisfaction in it, as though a healthy liberal democracy needed the occasional atrocity to justify itself. But in one form or another almost all the politicians interviewed in the immediate aftermath of the bombing said the same. It was the price – the terrible price – the country paid for its freedoms.

Did Fracassus think it was too high a price? All one can say for sure is that he tweeted **Terrible price to pay for freedom**.

Because of the outrage, the Prince and his party weren't allowed to leave the hotel that day. All three sat and watched the television in the hotel lobby in silence. Two hours after the bomb went off a terrorist group claimed responsibility. An hour after that the leader of a civil rights organisation warned against scapegoating the immigrant group whose ethnicity the terrorists shared. Already, Probrius nudged Fracassus into noticing, more concern had been expressed for the safety of the immigrant group than for the lives that had been lost. **Makes you wonder who the victims are**, Fracassus tweeted.

Dr Cobalt knew what Professor Probrius was doing and what Fracassus, under his tutelage, was struggling to give birth to as a thought. She seized a moment while Probrius was paying a visit to the lavatory to nudge Fracassus in another direction. 'This could have happened anywhere, you know.'

'Never has at home.'

'That doesn't mean it never will.'

'Couldn't happen in Cholm. Spravchik wouldn't let it.'

'You can't be sure of that.'

Probrius was back sooner than she'd calculated. It was possible he'd changed his mind, realising what she was shaping up to say to Fracassus.

The three exchanged suspicious glances in silence until Professor Probrius asked her how she would define a phobia.

'You know what a phobia is.'

'I want to hear it from your lips.'

'A phobia is an irrational fear.'

'What's irrational about a fear of being bombed?'

'Nothing. It's perfectly rational, unless it paralyses you from living your life.'

'Then what's irrational about being afraid of the people doing it?'

'Nothing. What's irrational is blaming everybody who looks like them.'

'Is it wrong to identify a source?'

'It is wrong to spread the net so wide that the source becomes an entire people.'

'How else, in a liberal democracy, are we to set about stopping it from happening again?'

'Increased security. Detective work. Intelligence . . .'

'And if they fail?'

'We have to try making the world a better place.'

'And in the meantime?'

'Act humanely.'

'And that means sympathising with the terrorists.'

'If it was terrorists who did it.'

'Oh, come on, Yoni, they've claimed it.'

'Ah, so now you trust them?'

'Ah, so now you don't?'

Fracassus, who had been attending to every word between them – it was the longest conversation he'd ever listened to from start to finish – tweeted underneath the table: **Liberal democracy equals more sympathy for bombers than for bombed**.

CHAPTER 21

The loneliness of the braggart

Never was a truer word spoken: A prophet is not without honour, save in his own land.

Far from his native country, where he had grown up in the shadow of his father the Grand Duke, Prince Fracassus was attracting attention for his ability to attract attention. With each new tweet and exploit another clipping was added to that collage of moral force and popular influence known to an age of rapid dissemination of trivia as personality. After his heroics at Gnossia, stories of the temple he was building in Cholm began to appear on message boards and news sites. A photograph of Cholm's Chief Minister, Vozzek Spravchik, anointing him with Numa oil high in the Blackbread Mountains with nothing but a drop into black infinity behind them, and soft round clouds like women's buttocks floating above, appeared again and again in celebrity magazines and colour supplements. Only an official selfie of the two men toe-wrestling in the barren Makindo Desert as the sun went down received more coverage – though that mainly in magazines for men who liked looking at photographs of men.

When his tweets on the subject of the Plasentza bombings appeared it was as though the prayers of thousands had been answered. The country did not lack for information and opinion. A liquid crystal display device in the hands of every citizen facilitated the transmission of all conceivable views on all conceivable subjects. Anything that could be said, had been said. But the digital context was everything: no one, especially in a liberal democracy such as Plasentza, wanted to see their thoughts or secret beliefs replicated word for word

on a hate site. Young himself, and photogenic in the sense that people were becoming accustomed to his image, Fracassus made available to the under-thirties what until now only the over-fifties had thought. By virtue of the family he came from, the title he held and the size of his property portfolio, he lent centrality to opinions hitherto only heard on the lips of disreputables and drunks. Though he could no more have strung his random vociferations into a system than he could have read a sentence of Thomas Carlyle on hero-worship, others had begun to marshal and codify everything he said for him. To those who argued that it hardly amounted to a political programme, others argued that it did. **Does/doesn't** was the stuff of Twitter and kept Fracassus's name before the public.

Occasionally at first, but with growing frequency, word of what he was saying leaked out of Plasentza back to the Republics. It began to be invoked in the course of those yoga-mat demonstrations which had been no more than a minor inconvenience for traffic at the time Fracassus left Urbs-Ludus, but had since grown into a serious threat to the stability not only of Urbs-Ludus but to All the Republics. 'Where is Fracassus?' was a call heard first on this side of the Wall, and then on that. '*Who* is Fracassus?' the Prime Mover of All the Republics was reported as enquiring. Though whether in fear of his influence or in expectation of his support no one could be sure.

Outside the Palace of the Golden Gates, few had known of Fracassus in his youth. He had not been allowed out into the world much. Brightstar intermittently championed him, but so ironically hyperbolic (unless it wasn't) had been their coverage that for every enthusiast they won to his cause, they lost a dozen. Now he was somewhere else, theories as to his true identity proliferated. He was an invention of a news-starved media. The House of Origen, having been shaken, first by the rumoured scandal of a sex-change heir, then by the demonstrations outside their properties, had come up with a manufactured robotic figure to mend their fortunes. Fracassus was a charlatan, a chimera, a ghost, a bankrupt. By the same token he was a businessman who turned to gold leaf everything he touched, an architect of wild dreams, a patriot, a hero, and an orator of genius.

That all this made him the ideal person to be given his own television show could not be disputed when the idea was floated to the Head of Celebrity at Urbs-Ludus Television. The word went out. Find him. Bring him back. Offer him anything.

But no one said 'immediately', so there seemed to be no hurry.

'Our boy is shaping up,' the Grand Duke told his wife.

'What as?'

'The thing we always wanted him to be. And quite frankly, if you take a look at what's happening on the street, the thing we need him to be.'

'I'm a mother, Renzo. A mother only wants her son to be happy.'

'He can be happy and great.'

'I still see his face on the day he left.'

Knowing his wife's aversion to their son's looks, the Grand Duke doubted that. 'Describe it to me.'

'He looked so sad.'

'It's good for someone his age to suffer disappointments.'

'Renzo, his whole world came crashing down.'

'He'd only known the girl ten minutes. I'd call that a brief disenchantment. Brief, but necessary.'

'You seem pleased it happened.'

The Grand Duke rose from his chair and paced the room. He did not like concealing things from his wife. 'My dear Demanska,' he said, 'I am pleased it happened and have no regrets that I made it happen. At the time he left us, Fracassus was, for all his stubbornness of character, a clay man. A person had only to graze him with their thumb and it left an impression that lasted for a month. It struck me as best to get some impressions over and done with while he was still young. I feel wholly vindicated by the figure he is cutting in the world right now.'

'You made it happen?'

'I did.'

'You hired a girl to break my son's heart?'

'Demanska, our son doesn't have a heart.'

'You actually paid someone?'

'Sojjourner, yes. I auditioned actresses but none could quite manage the self-righteousness. It turns out that only a Progressive Metropolitan Elitist can convincingly play a Progressive Metropolitan Elitist for money. I wanted Fracassus to fall for her and fall for her he did. I wanted him disillusioned and disillusioned he became. Now look at him. I made him so Progressive-proof that even Reactionaries start from his pronouncements.'

'And you know for sure the girl is not in his life somewhere?'

'They wouldn't last ten seconds in each other's company today.'

'Then I wonder who is in his life?'

'Ambition.'

'How lonely he must be.'

'You've forgotten how much he enjoys his own company. A vain man is never lonely. Which is a good job because a braggart never has a friend.'

'My poor Fracassus. How cruel you've been to him, Renzo.'

'Only to be kind, my dear. Only to be kind.'

He didn't tell her that the Head of Celebrity at Urbs-Ludus Television had been enquiring as to Fracassus's availability and mentioning eye-watering sums of money. Bearing her sensibilities in mind, he did suggest they think about giving Fracassus a book show, an idea they said they'd consider, though in such an event the fee would not be so eye-watering.

CHAPTER 22

In which the Prince forms an even higher estimate of his gifts

International communication having reached a level of sophistication and celerity unknown to previous ages, word of what the world was thinking of Fracassus reached him almost before it thought it. He would not have been human had this not moved him to what in a lesser person might have been called conceit, but in him passed as confirmation of abilities hitherto gone unremarked.

The bomb, he found the modesty to confess, had quickened his maturity. **I have gone from boy to man in a single morning**, he tweeted.

Within the week, newspaper supplements were carrying the story HOW A BOY BECAME A MAN, alongside photographs of mangled corpses. These he no sooner saw than he retweeted, and so there and back around the globe the message went as though it were the media equivalent of perpetual motion.

In the bomb, Fracassus saw – that is to say Professor Probrius taught him to see – not only his opportunity but a truth that offered opportunity for everyone. Society had grown degenerate. It had lost the ability to draw a distinction between the guilty and the innocent, it had lost the courage to blame, it had taken ordinary decent outrage and turned it into bigotry, it had made good people fear the consequences of their goodness. **Bombs only kill when we're scarred to kill the killer**, he tweeted.

That should be ***scared***, Professor Probrius told him. But it was too late.

Bombs only kill when we're scarred to kill the killer was re-tweeted more than a million times. **Scarred** was considered a master stroke, enmeshing in a visual, an auditory but, most important of all, a consequential way, the concepts of fear and wound, cowardice and disfigurement, the momentary and the never-to-be-forgotten. That which scared us scarred us. That which scarred us marked us out as scared. We who were afraid to condemn the bombers were also victims of their bombs. But where other victims died, we were only scarred, which made our being scared the more ignoble. Or was there something holy in our refusal to kill? Scared was an anagram of sacred, the anagrammatising clue being the verb to scar. Disfigure the word for afraid and we got the word for righteous.

There was no end to the play people could make of this mistake of genius.

'He's claiming it as his, I suppose,' Dr Cobalt said.

'He's trying to,' Professor Probrius replied. 'But he isn't quite sure what it is he's done. He came across the word anagram in a tweet the other day and had to put himself to bed. He's going in for a lot of jutting and pouting which is the usual sign he's bluffing something out.'

Whether Fracassus was aware of what he'd done or not, his name now hung in the firmament, fierce and vivid, like a hunter's moon. Invitations to him to return home and give a talk, a seminar, a lecture, anything he chose, flooded his mailbox. Caleb Hopsack congratulated his 'star Twitter pupil' and begged him to address the annual conference of the Ordinary People's Party. It took a while for the phlegmatic citizens of Plasentza to grasp that the tweeter of the hour, a real-live Prince and property tycoon who'd broken the spell under which they'd been living for decades, was actually resident in the capital city of their country. But once his presence had been verified they were eager to hear him. They hadn't realised how pusillanimous they were until, in 140 characters of fire, he'd shown them. They had practised tolerance for evildoers and tried to reintegrate them into society. They had cared for minorities and strangers, but now these same minorities appeared to them as self-pitying schismatics and those same strangers were planting bombs. What about their own needs? Who was speaking up for them?

Fracassus was.

Time to Muck Out the Pig-Pen, he tweeted, remembering a phrase his father had whispered into his crib.

Invited to discuss the Bomb as Opportunity at a meeting of the Plasentza Scientific and Philosophical Society, he drew huge crowds. He had feared he would have to make a speech of more than 140 characters and ordered Professor Probrius to write it for him, but the organisers assured him it would be enough if he simply mounted the rostrum and shouted 'Kill the killer.'

'Kill the killer,' the crowd chanted back.

'We're too scarred,' someone shouted. And then that too was picked up and passed from voice to voice.

Not knowing what to say, Fracassus turned his face sideways to the audience as he'd seen someone called Mussolini do in old newsreels. It was the very expression – though he could hardly be expected to remember that – with which he came into the world. He folded his arms and pursed his lips: a stance suggesting petulance on a Homeric scale. As though by divine chemistry, the audience was at once transformed into supplicants and Fracassus into a god who could stand there for eternity, waiting to be appeased. Nero, Mussolini, Fracassus.

'Frac-Ass-Us!' the people called.

Peevish and impassive, his fists clenched, Fracassus raised his chin and stared towards the east.

He left the stage still clenching his fists. Women fought to kiss his knuckles. 'Such a boy,' one said. 'And yet such a man,' said another.

'You haven't seen anything yet,' he told them.

'They haven't heard anything yet either,' Dr Cobalt muttered to Professor Probrius. They were standing to one side, waiting to escort him back to the hotel, not wanting to be seen. Fracassus was a prodigy. A monstrous and abnormal thing. He appeared from nowhere. It would disappoint the faithful to learn he had an elocution teacher and a life coach.

'He has a terrific advantage,' Probrius said, 'in that they don't actually come to hear him. There's something about him that compels attention. It can't be looks and it can't be presence, because he has neither.'

'Then what is it?'

'I think it's that very question. What is it? Why are we looking at him? He possesses the opposite to charisma to such a degree that people will stand for hours trying to figure out why they're standing there for hours.'

'But see how transfigured they look as they leave. It is as though they've been vouchsafed a vision.'

'They have. A vision of themselves. He is a mirror into their secret selves. They applaud their own words and leave transported.'

'He should go far.'

'He will.'

But first he had to address the Plasentza Chamber of Commerce.

Observing his reluctance – for Fracassus had been asked not to make his 'Kill the Killer' speech in deference to the feelings of businessmen who might have thought he meant them, and he couldn't remember what else he believed – Professor Probrius undertook to brief him, though his own understanding of business matters extended little beyond the conviction that the pursuit of money softened men's brains.

'Hardens them, you mean,' Dr Cobalt said one night, by way of pillow talk.

'I think that's your politics talking,' Probrius replied, supporting himself on one elbow. 'In my experience, those we call businessmen are the quickest of any profession to be impressed by the platitudes of success; to be dazzled by the prosaic financial exploits of one another; and to invest the most basic tricks of their trade, though they don't surpass the bartering of the schoolyard, with an unfathomable mystique. The whole science of business could be written on the back of a postcard.'

'You've never heard of the rich crushing the poor?'

'I have, my love. I have heard of it and observed it. But the cruellest of men can be gullible, and it is to tickle their gullibility that I am preparing the Prince.'

In which spirit he advised Fracassus . . .

To claim credit for what he hadn't done. To inflate figures. To make much of little. To drop names of people he didn't know. To invoke the sacred mysteries of the 'deal' and declare himself a master of its arts. To take delight in scoring the meanest of triumphs over the weakest of adversaries. To reverse the normal rules of polite society and brag about his worth. In short, to be himself.

How Fracassus beguiled an audience of bankers, fund-managers and developers three or four times his age, is the stuff of Plasentza business-community legend. How he told them that he owned more properties than in actuality he did. How he omitted all mention of his father and presented himself as a phenomenon of self-generation. How he told them, above their gasps of admiration, that he aimed high. How he told them that he thought big. How he made the shape of something big with his hands. How he divided life into those who push and those who allow themselves to be pushed, and how he was a pusher. How he told them that the first law of business was to know what you wanted, and how he told them that the second law of business was to make sure that you got it. How he told them that enriching oneself was godly but enriching oneself at the expense of others was very heaven. How he told them that he paid no taxes, for to pay tax only showed one ran one's business inefficiently. And therefore how he told them that he never would pay tax so long as there was a bone in his body . . .

As the audience of high-aimers and big thinkers rose to reward Fracassus with their admiration – for never had the things they thought found better expression – Professor Probrius counted himself satisfied.

'Didn't I tell you?' he told Dr Cobalt.

'To be proved right isn't always to be vindicated morally,' she said.

'You mean what's true shouldn't be true.'

'That's exactly what I mean.'

Vindicated morally or not, Probrius had to admit himself surprised by how well Fracassus's asseveration that he paid no tax was received, not only by the business leaders and captains of industry, but by the waiters and waitresses, the wine pourers, the glass polishers, the ushers, the security men, the sound engineers, and the members of the press. If the poorest of the poor had been here, Professor Probrius thought, they would have cheered with equal zest. Here, to all men, in an age of business, was the apotheosis of success: ONE WHO PAID NO TAX.

Yet again, Fracassus had his finger on the pulse.

Twitter, too, was busy that night.

Amazing guy. Remember to know what you want and get it. If only I'd known half of what he knows at his age. Amazing.

Inspirational, was another. **Think big! Aim high! Wow! Thank you, Prince Fracassus.**

CHAPTER 23

A short chapter with no lessons to be learnt therefrom

Though Prince Fracassus could sink slowly into oblivion for all Dr Cobalt cared, Professor Probrius was her lover and she was conjoined with him in his enterprise, however little she approved of it. She had to enquire, therefore, whether the Prince did not risk losing supporters from one level of society by his assiduous wooing of supporters from another.

Probrius understood her concerns but thought not. There was a universalism in the Prince's messages, he believed, which Yoni, who'd seen less of him close up, had not grasped. Take tax . . . But Yoni Cobalt would not even listen to what Probrius wanted to tell her. So far and no further, she told him. Tax was her red line.

Probrius laughed cynically. 'The road to hell,' he said, 'is paved with politicians' promises never to cross a red line. At least Fracassus would never make such a promise.'

'Promising not to make a promise to cross a red line is also a promise,' Yoni Cobalt said.

It so fell out that the Prince's next engagement was to judge a beauty pageant. Miss Plasentza. This time it was Professor Probrius who felt uneasy. He strongly advised the Prince against it. It was off-message, he said. You couldn't tweet **Bombs only kill when we're scarred to kill the killer** one minute, and then talk lipstick and deportment the next. But Fracassus knew his own mind. Judging a beauty pageant beat opening department stores and addressing groups of the hard of hearing.

'I'm very good with beautiful women,' he said.

Plasentza being a liberal democracy, its beauty contest was tolerated but not much approved of. It was held biennially in a small hotel on the outskirts of the capital and reported only on local radio. Fracassus agreed to participate on the understanding that the organisers booked the largest ballroom in the country, guaranteed the presence of television cameras, and gave him fifteen per cent of the take. Such was the fascination he engendered, his stipulations were met and his percentage increased to twenty.

He had lost much of his shyness. He could look women in the eye now. And not think they all looked like his mother. He had a metallic suit made for the occasion based on the one worn by Spravchik, and on the big night he inspected the contestants as he remembered the Minister inspecting the Numa women, getting the prettiest of them to twerk for him and then open their mouths to show him their teeth. He lowered his voice and asked each of them in turn if she was here only because she needed money to continue her studies. All but one said they wanted to be a model because the world needed beauty. The exception burst out crying. 'I can't believe that you can tell that about me,' she said. 'It shows,' he said, 'it shows.' He crowned her Miss Plasentza and backstage, after the show, made her cry again by pushing his hand down her dress.

BOMB BOY TYCOON BLOWS HIS TOP the *Plasentza Mail* reported. But it soon became clear that far from detracting from his burgeoning reputation, the assault helped it burgeon still more. He was a red-blooded young man. He meant what he did as a compliment not a rudeness. He had a love of loveliness in women and was expressing it.

A national debate followed. For many, this was a test case of liberal democracy itself. Enough was enough. People were tired of being told what they could and couldn't do, could and couldn't think, could and couldn't feel. They were fed up with having to feign pity every time the violation alarm was raised by some professional thin-skin who could weep and shake to order. So Fracassus had handled a woman's breast without remembering to ask her first! People who thought that was a crime needed to live in the real world where violence meant being held up at gunpoint in the food queue and sexism didn't stop at the misuse of a pronoun.

Women's magazines carried out polls of their readers. Ninety per cent of women in the lower ranks of society approved the Prince's action and said they wouldn't have minded in the least had he done it to them. It reminded some of them, fondly, of being wooed by their husbands. Fracassus tweeted that the ten per cent who disapproved were probably dogs. But he took no notice of any other figures. The people had spoken. The people were his people. And he was their man. **Great support**, he tweeted.

Sojjourner could fuck off.

'Unless you want to go on judging beauty pageants,' Professor Probrius advised, 'it might be time to think of moving on.'

Fracassus wasn't sure what Probrius had against him judging further beauty pageants.

'I don't think it's what your father had in mind for you.'

'He wanted me to see the world. I'm seeing it.'

But then he grew bored himself. There weren't that many beauty pageants to judge. Could that have been because there weren't that many beauties in Plasentza? 'Blame liberal democracy,' Dr Cobalt told him. 'The women here value things other than their appearance.'

Fracassus screwed up his face. 'What other things?'

'Intellectual development, careers, charitable causes, growing old gracefully.'

'Is that possible?' Fracassus asked.

'Intellectual development?'

'Growing old gracefully. I think women can be too old.'

'Too old for what?'

'Being a woman.'

'Don't tweet that, Your Highness,' Probrius advised.

Lacking the energy for a fight, Fracassus agreed. He had grown listless again. He sat in his room watching television. The world was talking about him but he wasn't talking about the world. There was nothing for him to do. He would have liked to build a casino or a chamber of horrors while he had time on his hands, but Plasentza had building regulations that Urbs-Ludus did not. He missed Spravchik. He missed women. He couldn't remember when he had last stood next to a woman who was taller than him. Probrius was right about liberal democracy and beauty – the more you got of the former, the less you got of the latter.

'What we could really do with,' he said one evening after dinner, 'is another bomb.'

And then, in a manner of speaking, one dropped.

CHAPTER 24

On the sadness of things. A son returns, a father prepares to depart

Mortality spares no one, let him build higher than a kite can fly. The Grand Duke fell ill.

It felt, to the people of Urbs-Ludus, like a sign. The Grand Duke was ill because the state was ill.

'Your father needs you,' Professor Probrius said. 'It's time to say your goodbyes and leave.'

A sadness descended on Fracassus. He realised he had no friends to say goodbye to. 'What have I achieved here?' he thought aloud. 'I haven't built a casino. I haven't wrestled. I haven't had much in the way of pussy.' (In fact he hadn't had any pussy but didn't want to admit that to himself.) 'The people love me, but I don't love them.'

He had heard there was a thing called depression. Could it be . . . ?

It was Dr Cobalt he turned to in matters of feeling. 'It's the lull before the storm, Your Highness,' she told him.

'I'm not asking about the weather,' Fracassus said. 'I'm asking about me.'

'It's the lull before *your* storm.'

Fracassus hated metaphors, without knowing what they were, almost as much as he hated foreign languages. 'What storm?'

Dr Cobalt, who had not had a great year herself, turned the screw. 'The éclat that's waiting for you when you return.'

What was waiting for Prince Fracassus on his return can be briefly stated. A dying father. A distraught mother. A flustered Palace. A restive populace. The possibility of war – for when trouble struck one of the Republics the others were unable to resist the opportunity to attack it. Air that had grown filthier in the time Fracassus had been away, though no more remarked upon than in the time he was there. Ditto, substituting heat for filth, the climate. A hunger for change. A dread of change. A virulent mutual distrust that pitted citizen against citizen. A passion for saying 'Love you' and appending smiley faces to messages expressive only of hate. Technological advance that had so far outstripped any human use for it that people were sending high-definition images of their faeces to imaginary acquaintances on the moon and watching others doing the same on screens they at all times carried in the palms of their hands. A belief in the free market of goods and ideas that concealed a profound reluctance to trade freely in either. A delight in what was gaudy that concealed a contempt for the wealth that made the gaudy possible. A contempt for wealth that concealed a veneration for it. A sense, that is to say, of universal futility and despair for which – and here was the part that interested the Prince – the only antidote was him.

Frac-Ass-Us!

The Republic was waiting for him.

All the Republics were waiting for him.

The Grand Duke received Professor Probrius in the Grand Boudoir. The room was decorated in the Grand Duchess's taste and so had fairies riding dragons on the walls and, to please her husband, dragons eating fairies on the ceiling. The mattress was fashioned to resemble a gold ingot and for all Probrius knew *was* a gold ingot. The duvet bore the Origen crest.

Professor Probrius made his deepest bow. 'I am sorry to see Your Highness brought low,' he said, 'but I trust the return of your beloved son will go some way to restoring your health. I believe you will find him much changed and ready for whatever you expect of him.'

The Grand Duke raised a frail hand. 'How the world loves a braggart,' he said in a frail voice.

'I hope you are not dissatisfied with the progress of his education,' Professor Probrius said. 'It goes without saying that neither I nor Dr Cobalt consider it to be finished.'

'We are more than happy,' the Grand Duke said. 'There are qualities of which my dear wife would have liked to see more. And others of which she would have liked to see less. But I confess myself satisfied. We entrusted a rough buffoon to your hands, and you have brought us back a polished one.'

Professor Probrius bowed again. 'And now, Your Highness?'

'And now the boy takes over from me as head of the House of Origen, and must prepare himself for the great leap forward. I confess it is all happening sooner than I anticipated and would like. He is young still. But my illness, together with the appeal his youth evidently exerts, combine to give this inevitability. History awaits us, Professor. There are already people below who, finally but fully cognisant of his gifts, are anxious to meet him and discuss how we proceed from here. The significance of this meeting, from their point of view and from ours, cannot be overstated; but time, I fear, is not on anyone's side. The streets are angry. We must proceed quickly. I am not strong enough myself to sit in on let alone superintend the discussions. I feel confident that your attendance will keep Fracassus focussed and ensure no liberties are taken with him. I have not seen the Prince since his return. I am weak and frankly find his company exhausting. He is said to have my eyes but I never did much like them. He is with his mother at the moment. Those in whose hands the destiny of the Prince and the House of Origen depend are in the Council Chamber on the ninetieth floor. Perhaps you will be so good as to repair there at once. Take Dr Cobalt with you. You have proved a formidable team. I will have the Prince join you presently, if he can tear himself from the bosom of his mother. He was suckled until his fourth year, you know. I put the formation of his character down to that.'

So saying, the Grand Duke fell back on to his pillows. Probrius feared the worse, but in fact His Highness was only sleeping.

It was with a great sense of purpose, to say nothing of a consciousness of history and honour, and therefore in a high state of nervous agitation, that Professor Probrius made his way to the ninetieth floor. He did not know who he was going to encounter in the Council Chamber, whether it would be the Prime Mover of All the Republics himself, or some of his most senior ministers, but the urgency with which the Grand Duke had prepared him clearly pointed to the imminence of a decisive political act – surely not a resignation in the Prince's favour, but why not a Cabinet position?

He texted Dr Cobalt. *Highest shoes*, he wrote. *And Quick*.

In fact she was already in the Chamber when he arrived, and deep in conversation with a person whose relaxed style of dress and free and easy demeanour declared him to be anyone but the Prime Mover.

'I might as well do the introductions, since I'm here,' Dr Cobalt said. 'Professor Probrius meet Lance Folder, Head of Celebrity for Urbs-Ludus Television.'

CHAPTER 25

'Stop it!'

Whether Prince Fracassus's distinguished television career could be said to grace the annals of politics or light entertainment was to remain a matter of controversy long after the Prince became what he became. It depended, to a degree, on the point of view of the disputants, and of course on how the Prince's rise to power, the reasons for it, and the resultant plusses or minuses of his 'reign', were viewed in toto.

Despite goodwill and alacrity on all sides, it took a fortuitous slip and then a fortuitous correction to get Fracassus on to the screen. Months were squandered, as the Grand Duke lay dying, debating such basic questions as what exactly it was that Fracassus could do, what his interests were, who would be his target audience, whether he was the stuff of daytime or night-time television, whether he should be scripted or spontaneous, and who, in the final analysis, would have creative control. That Fracassus had no interests, Professor Probrius and Dr Cobalt could have told the producers, but the latter had their own way of drawing the talent out and liked to make their own decisions as to watchability. In the end they reached, in this as in other matters, the same conclusions Dr Cobalt had come to years before. The Prince had no words and no interests and therein lay both his originality and – as could be attested to by the successes he had enjoyed on his travels – his popular appeal. What form to give this most rare of talents remained the stumbling block. Fracassus himself cited Spravchik as a model but Urbs-Ludus wasn't Cholm. Reality television was of necessity cruel, but there were guidelines, and handing your wife over to the secret police for stealing a flower from someone's garden breached all of them. The Prince's other idea was to make a contemporary reality version of *The Life and Loves of the Emperor Nero*, with himself taking the role of a latter-day emperor, and volunteers, of which there would surely be no shortage, playing Christians (or Muslims, Hindus or Jews – Fracassus was without prejudice). In the original, Nero dipped the Christians or whoever else in burning oil and then employed them as human candles to light his pool parties. The production team was quick to reject this suggestion, but on the grounds of cost rather than morality.

It sometimes happens that a title precedes a programme, indeed can be the inspiration for a programme, and so it proved to be in this case. In the months following his return to Urbs-Ludus, there gathered around the Prince – that is to say around the Prince's name – a sizeable representation of the Republic's youth, who discovered in his utterances much that found an echo in their own breasts and, even where his thoughts were unfamiliar to them, much with which they sought to make common cause. In their ebullience, they formed a cheer squad – Fracassites, they called themselves – wherever and on whatever subject the Prince spoke, threatening any members of the audience who showed the slightest inclination to disagree, or who even, by their lights, did not agree emphatically enough. At first they threatened violence without actually doing any. But imperceptibly, the mood of the meetings changed. Impressionable himself, Fracassus found an echo in his breast of the echo of him the Fracassites had found in theirs, and truth to say took pleasure in encouraging them. 'Chuck 'em out,' he'd shout, whenever the Fracassites lit upon dissenters, and in the mayhem that ensued – for no sooner did he shout 'Chuck 'em out' than everyone was shouting 'Chuck 'em out' – the odd bone was broken and a little blood was shed. The Grand Duke ordered Fracassus into his presence.

'This is not the way we do things,' he told his son. 'Put an end to it.'

Fracassus was disappointed. He'd seen professional wrestlers break more bones on breakfast television. But he couldn't countermand his dying father. 'What can I do?' he asked.

'It's not for me to tell you,' his father said. 'Have some human decency. And if you don't have any of your own, steal some.'

Fracassus thought hard and then addressed the Fracassites in a video link. 'Stop it,' he said, pointing a finger. He also put up posters in railway stations and at bus stops showing him mouthing the same words. 'Stop it.'

The phrase gained a sort of currency and finally reached the ears of the television production team. There it was, the thing they'd been looking for all these months. *Stop it!* Nobody else could deliver those words as Fracassus did. Nobody else could lay hold of so little in the way of moral indignation that what was intended as a reprimand came out sounding like an invitation. 'Stop it,' young men sidled up to women and whispered in their ears. And as often as not the stopping it went on through the night.

The moment the programme had a title it had a form. Fracassus would invite wrongdoers – wife-beaters, drug-takers, rapists, alcoholics, pickpockets, body snatchers, arsonists, forgers, cat burglars, paedophiles – to own up to their criminality, and then he'd tick them off for it. *Stoppit!* No outrage. No holier than thou condescension. No off-putting moralising. No warning or threats. And no bleeding-heart liberal connivance in the criminality either. Just *Stoppit!*

The advantage to Fracassus himself was obvious. He had only to say two words, and if he forgot those there was always autocue.

The show was an immediate success. It laid bare the immorality at the heart of society, sought neither to extenuate nor forgive, and then shrugged. Pinioned between moralists and apologists all their lives, the people tumbled on to their sofas, heaved sighs of relief that could be heard all over the Republic, and allowed Fracassus to disembarrass them of the ancient burdens of blame and absolution.

He was on their screens once a week, and then twice. If they watched repeats they could see him every other day. There were women to whom Fracassus's features were more familiar than their husbands'. Men thought of him as their friend. Children trusted him and would have leapt willingly into his black limousine had he pulled up to them in the street and offered them chocolate. *Stoppit!*

The day the Grand Duke died the papers carried the story that the father of Fracassus, the television personality, had *Stopped It*.

Professor Probrius and Dr Cobalt met in one of their old salad-bar haunts by the Wall and discussed what had transpired. They rarely saw the Prince now but he had retained their services out of some queer affection which they felt guilty about being unable to reciprocate. Occasionally he texted them regarding a word, but then either found another or changed his mode of expression. 'He's keeping us in reserve,' Professor Probrius said.

'Do you know what for?'

'I think he might be more insecure than we've ever realised. He could be wondering when he's going to run out of the ten words he uses and when, in that case, he'll need us again.'

'I think you flatter yourself.'

'Could be. But I've been right about everything so far.'

She spluttered into her salad. 'Right? What have you been right about?'

'Didn't I say that the secret of his success was failure?'

'No. I did.'

'Yes, but you were talking about *his* failure. I say the secret of his success is the failure of the people who look up to him. They want a hero who isn't there.'

'I said the first part of that. You said the second.'

'You/me – same difference. Man and wife are one flesh and all that . . .'

'Man and wife? Is that a proposal?'

'Could be.'

'Does that mean that the Prince has unwittingly brought us together? Can something come of nothing?'

'Is that a terrible thought?'

'Terrible.'

CHAPTER 26

Retards

With his father dead, there was no one in the way of Fracassus's rise, at least within the walled confines of Urbs-Ludus. His mother, who had spent increasing periods of time in her room, now never left it. As for his brother, no one knew where he was or would have recognised him had they known.

This situation released Fracassus into the fantasy that was himself. He bought up property, knocked it down or built it higher, as the fancy took him. He put casinos into poorhouses and strip clubs into old people's homes. From the sky, the Republic of Urbs-Ludus had begun to take on a magical quality, so vertiginous were Fracassus's towers and so extravagant their illumination. From the ground it was now impossible to see a single star. **You're lucky if you get to see the moon these days**, the architecture critic for the *Urbs-Ludus Guardian* wrote. **You'll be seeing the moon and the stars when I knock the crap out of you**, Fracassus tweeted in response.

At get-togethers of the Fracassites, 'Knock the crap out of 'em' replaced 'Chuck 'em out' as the *cri de rage*, no matter that there was no actual person among them to rage against.

Sometime towards the end of his third series of *Stoppit!* the producers called Fracassus in for a serious conversation about its future. 'If you're planning to axe me I'll sue the shit out you,' he announced before he'd even taken off his coat. They weren't planning to axe him. Quite the opposite. So good were the viewing figures for *Stoppit!* that they'd been searching for a follow-up show. As ever, it was finding a good title that had held things up. But now they had it. The mystery was why it had taken them so long. *Starttit!* How good was that? *Starttit!* – in which young entrepreneurs, some of them perhaps reformed malfeasants from *Stoppit!* (television loved to recycle) would confide their business hopes and dreams to Fracassus and he would show them how they could be realised. Who knew better about starting a business than he, a penniless child from the shadow of the Wall who had clawed his way out of obscurity to light the sky up with his name? Everyone knew that Fracassus was born a prince and given his own ziggurat every birthday, but the lie was so preposterous it was charming, and besides, everyone wanted to believe it. The lie that the Grand Duke Fracassus had made himself out of nothing allowed the people to believe that they could make themselves out of nothing too. In the flagrancy of the falsehood they found a new spirituality of material hope.

And this was not a Sunday morning spirituality, gone when the working week began. Believers could now watch *Stoppit!* on a Monday, Tuesday and Thursday, and *Starttit!* on a Wednesday, Friday and Saturday. Meaning there would be only one day when he was not on the screen – Sunday, the day of lesser faiths, the day the people rested from Fracassus and missed him.

The one disadvantage of Fracassus's new show, viewed from where he stood, was that he'd have to speak more. He called back Professor Probrius, who'd prepped him for his address to the Plasentza Chamber of Commerce. Could Probrius remember any of the things Fracassus had said on that occasion. Professor Probrius consulted his notes. 'You advised, Your Highness, to aim high, think big, stay focussed, never quit, push hard, laugh at retards, and pay no tax.'

'That,' the Grand Duke Fracassus said, 'should get me through the first series.'

Soon, between *Stoppit!* and *Starttit!* there was little else on television that anyone wanted to watch. Even Fracassus wondered what he'd be watching if he wasn't watching himself. And then, in the best spirit of reality shows, television broke a story about itself. Halfway through a live breakfast programme a gang of masked men and women burst into the studio – the very studio in which *Stoppit!* and *Starttit!* were made – narrowly failing to kill Fracassus. In fact they invaded on his day off, so strictly speaking they didn't narrowly miss killing him at all. Nor were they carrying any weapons to kill him with. But the implication was there for anyone to see. Fracassus stood for free speech and these brigands stood for the opposite. Exactly what happened was not clear, no matter that the entire Republic watched it live, but the short and the long of it was that the masked raiders shouted 'Bang!', ordered the presenter and the studio manager to put their hands above their heads, and took them and a young make-up artist hostage.

Who they were; where they had come from; how they had breached security; what they wanted; who shouted 'Bang!' first; what could have been done to prevent the attack; what could be done to prevent it in the future – these were some of the questions to which the people, watching the event unfold before their eyes, demanded answers.

Nothing of this kind had ever happened in Urbs-Ludus or any of the other Republics before. Had the toy gunmen been nationals their motives would have been easier to fathom. Everyone was angry about something. Everybody was trailing in the wake of someone else. The entire population was but a breath away from marching into a television studio and demanding justice. But these belligerents were not nationals. They had dark skin, black hair and even when they only shouted 'Bang!' they shouted it in an alien tongue that made the blood curdle. Once accept that they were foreigners there were still more questions to be answered. The Republic was peaceable to the point of docility. It had no weapons, no history of colonial adventurism, and no international ambitions beyond inviting visitors to go up and down in lifts with golden doors. It had made no compromising alliances, and to tell the truth had no foreign policy of any sort.

Half an hour into the raid, the attackers took off their masks, revealed themselves to be artisans and demanded, if they were to release their hostages, an end to the opprobrium in which they and their families were held. It wasn't so long ago that they'd been applauded into the country. Now, the same people who had cheered them at the railway stations, were booing them in the street. Even sales of artisanal breads had slowed.

See the matter from their side and they were victims. See it from the point of view of frightened hostages and viewers expecting to catch the news on television and they were common criminals. **Knock the crap out of 'em**, Fracassus tweeted.

Whether, with that one tweet, Fracassus – the best-known television personality in the Republics and the owner of the twelve highest towers – taught the people what to think, or whether he simply found himself in accord with the popular mood, is a distinction that only history can make. Suffice it to say that he at once became the mouthpiece for a party that did not as yet exist. Whoever believed that the artisans should be arrested for betraying the trust and hospitality of their hosts, waterboarded, horsewhipped, humiliated and shot by firing squad knew themselves to be of the party of Fracassus and that, by the mathematics of rage and vengeance, meant the majority of the people. The Prime Mover of All the Republics, sensing public anger grow but conscious of his government's obligations to international law, sent in a soft force to break the siege. The artisans surrendered without a fight. They would now be tried in accordance with local law. Should they be found guilty of affray – and the Prime Mover was prejudging nothing – they would be returned to their countries of origin, always provided, of course, that their countries of origin would deal humanely with them on their return. The statement was ill-timed. On the day of its issue, the young make-up artist, though now released and at home, suffered a belated panic attack. Fracassus put out a numbered series of tweets.

(1) **Justice in our time? Some justice!**
(2) **The guilty sent home like heroes.**
(3) **The victims returned to their loved ones in body bags.**

That a body bag was coming it a bit thick as a description of someone prescribed mild antidepressants, only a few literalists bothered to point out. The Republic's blood was up. People who had been tweeting **Chuck 'em out** had suddenly to rephrase their outrage. **Keep 'em here**, they tweeted, **so we can knock the crap out of 'em. Then chuck 'em out.**

On small events rests the fate of nations. The artisanal invasion of the television station was one of those hairspring moments when you could hear history teeter on the wire. Fracassus felt something even bigger than history – fate, destiny, the hour – run like fire through his veins. The Prime Mover must have felt the same thing drain clean away. There were angry demonstrations outside the Executive Building. People made effigies of him – no matter that no one knew what he looked like – and set fire to them in public parks. Every rioter found common cause with every other. They wanted different things but more than anything else they wanted something. For every tweet supporting the Prime Mover there were a thousand – many, it is true, written by Fracassus – calling for him to resign. So one day in the dead of winter, perspiring heavily, resign was exactly what he did.

Outside the Palace of the Golden Gates, demonstrators calling to disband all working groups on climate change joined demonstrators calling to raise the age of consent for homosexuals and together they called for Fracassus.

He appeared briefly on the Palace steps under a canopy of gold. 'We're going to Muck Out the Pig-Pen,' he promised.

'You *are* the Pig-Pen,' someone shouted.

Fracassus located him and pointed. 'Retard,' he told the crowd, shaking his head as though to ask what could be done about a world that had such retards in it, and then, to their delight, he did his old imitation of a spastic marionette.

Watching from an upper window which no sound could penetrate, Dr Cobalt guessed Fracassus had finally gone too far. She couldn't say she was sorry.

Professor Probrius, standing behind her, kissed the nape of her neck.

'I see the nature of the electorate still eludes you,' he said. 'The word retard is a great bonder.'

Had she bothered to look out of the window again, Yoni Cobalt would have seen 500 Fracassus supporters all being spastic marionettes.

CHAPTER 27

In which Fracassus proves he is no longer in love

Mighty would be the pen, and nimble the hand wielding it, that could do justice to the speed of events that now overtook the Republics – not only the physical aspects of a dissolution and the setting of dates for an election, but the invisible perturbations: the turbulence felt in every breast at the prospect of they knew not what, the wild gossip, the recriminations, the horrid prognostications on all sides, the told-you-sos from people who had told no one anything unless reading the extreme weather as a portent of troubles ahead could be called a something. Now add to this the foment into which the intellectual life of the Republics was thrown, first by the news that Fracassus had, indeed, as was expected, tossed his hat into the ring as a House of

Origen Independent, and then by the rumours that an unknown PhD student called Sojjourner Heminway would stand for the Progressive Party on a platform that embraced equally the desire for something different and the need for everything to stay the same. Everyone had heard of Fracassus. No one had heard of Sojjourner. And yet somehow everyone felt they had. Heminway . . . Heminway . . . Ahead of any formal announcement, the news was leaked that she was the great-great-granddaughter of someone else no one had heard of at the time, but who turned out to be the great-great-granddaughter of the Republics' very first Prime Mover. Prime Movers of All the Republics were rarely seen and never remembered, but a Prime Mover was still a Prime Mover and the fact that Sojjourner Heminway had the first Prime Mover's blood in her veins lent to her challenge, if and when she made it, the gravitas of continuity. Soon, if and when became yes and then. But simultaneous with confirmation of her candidacy came the announcement that she was launching a campaign to save the Artisanal Seven as they were now to be designated. They had play-acted their protest, she argued, in deference to the frolicsomeness of Urbs-Ludus. It had been a prank with a purpose. They had voiced their grievance in a public place, in a spirit of fun, and while they didn't seek to absolve themselves of responsibility for distress and injury, none of that had been their intention. In its own way, too, their demonstration highlighted the cultural impoverishment into which a sequence of illiberal administrations had allowed the nation to fall. One of the charges brought against the Artisanal Seven was that they disrespected the Republics' prime source of entertainment and information. But it was they, the artisans, who deserved our respect, firstly for the changes they had wrought to the culinary arts in Urbs-Ludus – both as to the taste of food and as to its appearance – and secondly for the mellifluous languages that could now be heard pleasing the ear in every corner of the once monolingual Republics. What was television to this? Television, with its endless repeats of cheap programmes bought from outside the Walls and even cheaper repeats of reality programmes whose only beneficiary was the ego of the millionaires to whom it gave prominence. She spoke of millionaires in the plural so as not to personalise her argument too soon, but everyone knew to whom she was referring. The election had not begun and already it was turning toxic.

Fracassus was thrown into confusion by the reappearance of the only woman ever to have almost touched his heart. His widowed mother believed this second coming of the wickedly Elitist witch to be an omen, and warned her son to withdraw from a race which, in the way of mothers, she didn't think he had a cat in hell's chance of winning. He told her he could barely remember who Sojjourner was and resorted to Twitter. **May the best man win**, he tweeted, by way of allusion both to Sojjourner's gender and her trousers, but Caleb Hopsack, making a sudden intervention, advised him against too early an assault on Sojjourner Heminway's appearance. It would be politic, in his view, for Fracassus to keep his powder dry and not accuse his rival of lacking a dress sense appropriate to the position of Prime Mover until much closer to polling day. That would be the best time, too, to insinuate that only lesbians never wore dresses. She would be tired and emotional by then and less able to defend herself. Fracassus didn't have to be told twice. He had seen enough fights to know that the real killer blows were those landed in round fifteen. I agree with you, he told Hopsack and tweeted **Anyone think she has the stamina for this? I don't, I don't**.

The other thing he did, to let Sojjourner know she was fooling herself if she believed he thought about her still, was to find himself a wife. This he achieved by travelling incognito to the Nowhere Palace and selecting the croupier who looked most like his mother, reasoning that whoever looked most like his mother looked least like

Sojjourner. He wrote her name down on a piece of paper so that he wouldn't forget it and married her by special decree the day after. Caleb Hopsack, whose wardrobe Fracassus still longed to emulate, was his best man.

Not wanting the grass to grow beneath his feet, Hopsack followed up on his advice regarding Sojjourner Heminway's appearance with a visit to the Palace, in the first place to offer Fracassus his condolences – Fracassus could not at first remember what there was for him to be condoled about – and in the second to volunteer his services as Campaign Manager with Special Responsibilities for Twitter which, as anyone with political nous now understood, had grown to be as significant in the winning of votes, if not in the changing of minds, as the stump speech and the rally. Fracassus had embraced his old mentor, wondered where he had been, didn't listen to the answer, installed him in the very position he'd requested and asked him to be his groomsman. Hopsack accepted and had himself photographed again outside the Golden Gates. It was while he was fumbling for the ring that he learned of one limitation to his power. 'I want Philander to share responsibility with you for the media campaign,' Fracassus whispered, before turning to the marriage officiant and affirming, 'I do.'

Caleb Hopsack expressed reservations about Philander at the reception. 'You never know where he's going to be or what he's going to say,' he said.

'I see that as an advantage,' Fracassus replied. He had chosen cord trousers the same canary yellow as his hair, and a brown and purple windowpane check jacket with four vents, to be married in. Unsure of Palace protocol, Caleb Hopsack had come in tails.

Fracassus emailed Philander under the table while his new wife was making her speech. *Need you.*

Accipio cum gaudio, Philander emailed back.

Caleb Hopsack stole a look at Fracassus's phone. 'Ordinary people are not going to be pleased with too much of that,' Caleb Hopsack told him from the side of his mouth.

'Then there's your first job,' Fracassus said. 'You stop him.'

'You've just started him.'

'I know.'

Fracassus had hatched a plan. He was going to be an enigma.

Fracassus had not met Philander since the time he came down off the bus and told him to believe every word he said – that's to say to disbelieve all of it – not because it was true but because it wasn't. For his part, Philander had no memory of that meeting. 'I forget everybody I meet,' he confessed, when the two men got together at the Palace, 'because I'm not interested in them.'

'I am exactly the same,' Fracassus said.

What he wanted Philander to do was organise buses to tour the Republics making promises that could never be kept, those being the sorts of promises the populace preferred. Philander flicked the hair out of his eyes and made a salute. 'Roger,' he said. Then he made a joke – 'Mind you, I'm not promising.'

Fracassus, who had never got a joke, didn't get this one. But he trusted Philander to let him down. In his eyes the campaign was now well and falsely up and running.

Artisanal Seven! Fracassus tweeted. **Losers.**

Hopsack texted his dissatisfaction. *Public want action not insults.*

Artisanal Seven! Fracassus texted. **Chuck the losers out.**

Not quite there yet, Hopsack tweeted. *Something more definite required. Public wants assurances there won't be more.*

I will build a wall, Fracassus tweeted. **And when I build a wall no one gets over it.**

Better, Hopsack texted. *But 'no one gets* **in**' *would be better still. 'Over' suggests athleticism and ordinary people like that. 'In' suggests invasion and ordinary people fear that.*

But by that time the wall had gone viral. **Build the wall! Build the wall!** 20,000 people tweeted in ten minutes.

Sojjourner's team tweeted that there already was a wall.

Oops! Fracassus retorted. **They think they've got me. Well I'm gonna build a higher wall.**

In another ten minutes another 20,000 tweeters. **Build a higher wall! Build a higher wall!**

Sojjourner was not above tweeting below the belt herself. **Inanity can do as much damage as malignancy**, she posted. And followed this with a caricature of Fracassus, Hopsack and Philander posing together in front of the Golden Gates. **Money, imposture and humbug**, she tweeted. **The Three Wise Monkeys of Urbs-Ludus. Screw the Economy, Screw the People, Screw the Weather.**

Fracassus couldn't have been happier. The words Sojjourner used were too long. Inanity! Malignancy! Imposture! Whoever kept a friend, never mind won an election, saying 'imposture'? He practised pronouncing it in front of a mirror, pouting his lips as though to kiss an old lady from the other side of the room. He looked forward to using it in the forthcoming television debate.

She accused him of profiteering, sexism, mendacity (another one), racism, incitement to hatred, isolationism, and bad spelling.

He accused her of inexperience, liberal elitism, political correctness, man-hating, minority mania, and softness on terrorism. She was not a person, he went on, to be trusted with her finger on the nuclear button. 'Finger' was the only word in that list that was his.

She accused him of not knowing that the Republics didn't have a nuclear button.

I wouldn't worry about that, Caleb Hopsack texted him to say. *The Ordinary People's Party have been campaigning to maintain our nuclear capability for years. They won't want to be told we don't have one.*

Philander sent Fracassus an email from one of the neighbouring Republics, he wasn't sure which. *Confusion all confounded this end. Electorate don't know what to think so I'm telling them not to think anything. Regarding nuclear button, press the young harridan on her ignorance of defence issues. Say there is button but only you know where to find it. Bonam fortunam.*

She accused him of being in bed with the military.

He accused her of being in bed with no one.

Don't go there, Hopsack texted.

Fracassus amended his tweet and accused her of wanting to be in bed with him.

No! Hopsack texted.

She accused him of toe-wrestling with foreign autocrats.

He accused her of xenophobia, a word Philander had emailed him.

Again no! Hopsack texted.

She accused him of putting the interests of his business empire before the interests of the country.

He accused her of confusing the country with her class and of giving succour to extremists. (Philander again.)

You're falling into her trap, Hopsack texted. *Stick to words of one syllable or she'll pull you down with her.*

Like Leander enticing Hero, Philander added by email.

Dr Cobalt entered the conversation, contesting that version of the myth. Hero swam to Leander of his own accord.

Professor Probrius agreed, but thought the story open to innumerable interpretations.

Start opening that door, Dr Cobalt argued, and there was no saying what moral and behavioural relativism wouldn't amble through it next.

Losing plot, Hopsack texted. *Get rid of those two.*

Fracassus was surprised to discover himself sentimentally attached to his old tutors and fired them on the spot.

CHAPTER 28

A brief treatise on buffoonery

Much as Philander knew better than anyone that life was a sore trial and man's tenure of it brief, he was still taken aback when he too was dismissed from Team Fracassus. Though Caleb Hopsack had always been against Philander's appointment, he wasn't the person directly responsible for the dismissal. Whichever way one looked at it, that person was Philander himself.

It began with a picture in a newspaper – it doesn't matter which, since it appeared eventually in all of them – of two otters whose recent acquisition by Urbs-Ludus Zoo caused greater interest than it might otherwise have done on account of their extraordinary resemblance, both in body and in face, to Fracassus and Philander, after whom they were instantaneously named. In the photograph, the Fracassus otter had his head to one side, much as Fracassus would incline his whenever a subject beyond his comprehension arose and he wanted to show his disdain for it. Despite the reputation for cuteness enjoyed by the species, this otter showed his teeth in unexplained fury. When his mother saw the photograph it brought immediately to mind Fracassus's expression the time he came into the bedroom she shared with her dear late husband, turned his mouth into a trumpet of hate, and said 'Fuck, nigger, cunt.' The other otter, forever to be known as Philander, possessed the original's genius for looking at once serious and amused and delighting in his capacity to be both. He was carrying a fish in his mouth, boastfully, as though no other otter in the sea had ever fished as well as he had, and this too reminded people of Philander. The photograph was captioned Maccus and Fracassus – Maccus being a character in a popular children's movie of long ago, a villain with a head resembling that of a hammerhead shark, and Fracassus being Fracassus.

Philander, being Philander, felt the need to go into print at once, firstly to show that he got the joke and enjoyed it, and secondly to discourse on the name Maccus which went back a lot further than *The Pirates of the Caribbean*, first appearing as the designate for a stock figure of ancient Roman farce, not to be confused with Buccus who, in Philander's view, was funnier. Perhaps without his actually knowing it, the journalist responsible for the otter story had started a conversation about the nature of buffoonery as differently understood by the ancients and the moderns, indeed as bearing widely differing interpretations today. To note a resemblance between the Grand Duke Fracassus and him was inevitable given their close political connection, and without doubt flattering to himself, bearing in mind his subordinate position. But while they were both buffoons, the buffoonery of the one was not to be confused with the buffoonery of the other. His own, if he would be permitted to say so, was entirely self-aware – an act of conscious self-disparagement aimed at puncturing his own and society's pomposity and preventing people from confusing levity with falsehood – whereas Fracassus's proceeded from too deep an engrossment in the cares of office for him to notice he was being ridiculous or be concerned about it. Where he, Philander, was the author of his own buffoonery, Fracassus was its victim. But let us not despair! The great Plato, it should never be forgotten, had abhorred a sense of humour in a ruler, by which logic, as a person entirely lacking in one, the Grand Duke Fracassus was a more natural leader, Platonically speaking, than he, Philander, would ever be.

Called to explain this, Philander pleaded loyalty. What else was he saying but that Fracassus was ideally suited for the role of solemn majesty that awaited him? But wriggle on the pinhead as he might, Philander stood accused of calling the man whose election he was meant to be working for a clown. And an inferior clown, at that, to his accuser. He had to go. *Acta est fabula*, he wrote in his goodbye email to Fracassus. The play is over – though it wasn't so far over that Philander had no further part to play in it. Before the day was out he was working for Sojjourner Heminway.

CHAPTER 29

The speed of lies

Grievous as Philander's defection might have been, it wasn't. Nor was he the only recreant in the months leading up to the election. Of Fracassus's original team, only Caleb Hopsack remained. Ideologically, Hopsack felt at one with Fracassus. The Grand Duke and the leader of the Ordinary People's Party – it was a marriage of converging interests made in political-convenience heaven. Hopsack attended the Palace every morning, was photographed with or without Fracassus in front of the Golden Gates, and brought news from the remotest corners of the Republics. Good news and bad, though it was easy – as with the Philander affair – to confuse the two. It was Hopsack who, as a politician incapable of inspiring loyalty himself, best understood why the people loved those whom no one else could. Where the Sojjourner camp took comfort from the spectacle, as they saw it, of rats deserting a sinking ship, the populace saw a beleaguered leader betrayed by inferior men. Fracassus had promised to Muck Out the Pig-Pen. Well, these were the squeals the Pigs made when they resisted eviction. Rats, pigs – who needed them? The fewer influential followers Fracassus had, the more honourable they believed him to be. Other politicians could boast their lickspittles and cronies. Fracassus stood alone. His isolation proved his authenticity.

Authenticity became the word of the campaign. At least he says what he means, Hopsack's people tweeted. And saying what one meant became more important than meaning what one said.

Sojjourner no sooner secured Philander's services than she wished she hadn't. What she'd hoped would be a public relations coup turned into its opposite. Was she so desperate that she needed Fracassus's cast-offs? Was she so lacking in integrity herself that she was indifferent to its absence in others? Quick to see her mistake, she sent Philander to tour the remotest corners of the Republic on a bus, from which he made exactly the same speeches he'd made when he was working for Fracassus.

Otherwise, Sojjourner's operation appeared to be on track. 'Appeared to be' in the sense that pollsters showed her enjoying a healthy lead over her opponent, no matter that her rallies were less populous and ecstatic. The website Brightstar, which had been on Fracassus's side ever since his birth, read the polls as a Liberal conspiracy to keep Fracassus out and saw her unenthusiastic rallies as the true measure of her unpopularity. She was too dumpy to be liked, it said, too small to be seen, too shrill to be listened to, too cold to excite hope, too excitable to calm fears, too assertive to be womanly, too remote from the struggles of ordinary people, too close to a pampered elite, too ambitious, too pushy, too ready to play the woman card, though, frankly, anyone less like a woman . . . and much else in that vein.

If it didn't say that she was too clever for her own good it was only because it didn't want to invite comparisons with Fracassus, who was definitely clever enough for his.

With only a few weeks of the election left to run, Fracassus believed it was time to mention her trousers. **Those trousers**, he tweeted.

That jacket, Sojjourner's people tweeted back.

But the trousers were more telling.

Professional commentators wondered if she'd turn up for the televised debate in a slit skirt and stilettos. There was little doubt that this would put Fracassus on the back foot. It was well known that a slit skirt could induce catalepsy in Fracassus. **Only on the right woman**, he tweeted, when this matter was raised publicly. Whatever his protestations, who could say, if Sojjourner were to wear a skirt, that Fracassus, guided by a power greater than himself, wouldn't attempt to slide his hand under it?

Sojjourner scotched all such expectations in advance by insisting that while light entertainment, or whatever name he gave to groping women, might be his field of operations, serious politics was hers. Election watchers called this her first mistake of the night. At a stroke she took the fun out of the debate and showed that she was out of touch with the times. People, even of her class, had grown weary of gropee victimology. Frankly, no one cared where Fracassus put his hands. Her second mistake was to mention the glass ceiling. So what if no other woman in history had ever made it to be Prime Mover? People weren't going to be gender-bullied into making her the first. Her third mistake was to invoke diversity, a concept interpreted by voters to mean people of every sexual orientation and colour but their own. To be white and straight in Urbs-Ludus, when Sojjourner was at the stump, was to feel neglected. Her fourth mistake was to use the word 'imposture', enabling Fracassus, who couldn't believe his luck, to purse his lips in practised imitation of its prissiness and make as though to kiss an old lady from the far side of the room. Looking directly into camera he mouthed the words 'Stop it!', at one and the same time mocking his opponent's verbosity and reminding viewers that it was he who owned the medium that fed their fantasies. Her fifth mistake, which could be said to encompass all the others, was to oppress viewers with her mastery of argument and comprehensive grasp of world affairs.

Watching on a television in Yoni Cobalt's apartment, Kolskeggur Probrius savoured the delicious irony of it. In the days of the Great Purge of the Illuminati, Sojjourner Heminway had been one of the students instrumental in getting him removed from the university for demeaning those he taught by teaching them too well. Now here she was, falling foul of just such contempt for knowledge herself, only this time the judges were the common people not the privileged elite. The great purge of the purgers had begun.

Yoni Cobalt sat with her head in her hands all through the debate and kept them there as the first verdicts on the candidates' performances were delivered.

'I won't say I told you so,' Professor Probrius said. 'But I did long ago predict that those who tell the stories run the world.'

'Stories! What stories? He doesn't have anything to tell.'

'My love, that *is* the story.'

Thus, without saying a word, and in losing the debate by every known measure, Fracassus was deemed to have won it.

Greatest margin of victory in any televised debate in history, he tweeted.

And then again, an hour later, **Time to send sad Sojjourner on a long jjourney.**

CHAPTER 30

The end of days

It has been observed that mankind plays at life and only realises the seriousness of what it's done when it's too late.

In the days immediately preceding the election a baffled stillness fell on the Republics, and on Urbs-Ludus, the play capital, in particular. What, of all that had been said, did anybody mean?

There'd been a change of mood after the debate. Fracassus had won by not winning but didn't act or look like a winner in the days following. He oozed belligerence in his tweets, but on his person an unaccustomed softness could be discerned. Caleb Hopsack's heart beat faster. He feared that Fracassus had suddenly developed an interior life, a dangerous black hole that could suck in self-doubt and second thoughts. Caleb Hopsack might have been a joke that only the smartest people got, but to himself he was certitude or he was nothing. Without it, the ground he walked on felt like the surging sea. There was terror in his tweets. **Beware the backsliders**, he tweeted, not just once but a hundred times. If the world slid back he would be the first to be engulfed. He pictured himself face down in the landslipped mud, where he would lie uncorrupted by change for 100,000 years until some fresh-faced archaeologist found him and wondered what function such a creature, strangely garbed and grimacing, could ever have performed.

Fracassus visited his mother in her chocolate factory and fairy room. She too thought there was something different about him. For a moment she even saw how it might be possible to like him. She asked him how his wife was handling the pressure. He looked bemused. He had forgotten he had a wife. He surprised her by enquiring about his brother. Had she heard from him recently? Normally he referred to Jago as 'It'. Today Jago was his brother. It was a self-centred enquiry, but it was an enquiry all the same. Did he say anything about the election, he wondered. 'I cannot lie to you,' his mother said. 'He will be voting for Sojjourner.' She was surprised that Fracassus was not angered by this. 'I don't blame him,' he said. 'I'd do the same in his position.'

On his way out he tried guessing how many transpersons there were in the Republics. He reckoned he could afford to lose them all and still romp home a comfortable winner. But he didn't tweet to say so.

Whatever had softened Fracassus, softened the populace. Not to the point of persuading those who hated Sojjourner to change their minds and vote for her. A change of mind is a rational decision and hatred of Sojjourner had nothing of reason in it. It was fed from wells of poison too deep to fathom. But it was as though belief in Fracassus began to blow away, like leaves that had only ever rested on him lightly. An hour before they'd been at the pantomime shouting 'She's behind you!' Now that they were back out on the street it was as though the pantomime had been watched by someone else.

Though they were frightened to disrupt the stillness, the yesterday men and women of Fracassus's diatribes – the educated, the knowledgeable, the sad, the losers, the Metropolitan retards – dared to let hope penetrate their bunkers. It had all been a fiction. Even Fracassus didn't seem to believe any of it really. All men have some goodness in them, don't they, let it only be an inadvertent mote blown out of someone else's eye. It was a salutary warning. Fracassus had been sent to frighten them out of their complacency. This thing could happen. I'm behind you. Mind your backs.

Very well. They'd learnt their lesson. They were listening. The people had given them a second chance. In the darkest hours, it was always the people who shone the brightest. Look, and you could see a streak of light. Listen, and you could hear sanity returning to the Republics like water returning to a dried-up riverbed. The sad bought in extra champagne. The losers invited their friends around to party. The retards danced their little disjointed dance.

But then the wind seemed to turn again. Leaning out of Yoni Cobalt's window on election night, Kolskeggur Probrius wet his finger.

Yoni Cobalt felt the muscles in his back tense and then relax.

'What?' she said.

He didn't turn around. He didn't have the heart to tell her what he knew.